Katya's Gold

What Will Her Dreams Cost?

To order additional copies of *Katya's Gold*,
by Ellen Bailey, call **1-800-765-6955**.

Visit us at **www.reviewandherald.com**
for information on other Review and Herald® products.

Guide PRESENTS

Katya's Gold

What Will Her Dreams Cost?

REVIEW AND HERALD®
PUBLISHING ASSOCIATION
Since 1861 | www.reviewandherald.com

Published by Review and Herald® Publishing Association,
Hagerstown, MD 21741-1119

Review and Herald® titles may be purchased in bulk for educational, business, fundraising, or sales promotional use. For information, please e-mail SpecialMarkets@reviewandherald.com.

The Review and Herald® Publishing Association publishes biblically-based materials for spiritual, physical, and mental growth and Christian discipleship.

The author assumes full responsibility for the accuracy of all facts and quotations as cited in this book.

This book was
Edited by Penny Estes Wheeler
Designed by Ron J. Pride
Cover art by Kim Liddiard/thecreativepixel.com
Interior designed by Heather Rogers
Typeset: Goudy 13/16

PRINTED IN U.S.A.

12 11 10 09 08   5 4 3 2 1

Library of Congress Cataloging-in-Publication Data
Bailey, Ellen.
   Katya's gold : what will her dreams cost her? / Ellen Bailey.
      p. cm. -- (A guide true story book)
   Summary: Growing up in communist Ukraine in the late twentieth century, Katya Anatolyevna feels out of place until she becomes a cross-country skier, which eventually leads her not only to compete in the Olympics, but to join the Adventist Church.
   ISBN 978-0-8280-2335-1
   1. Anatolyevna, Katya--Juvenile literature. 2. Seventh-Day Adventists--Biography--Juvenile literature. 3. Cross-country skiing--Ukraine--Biography--Juvenile literature. I. Title.
   BX6193.A53B35 2008
   286.7092--dc22
   [B]
                                    2007049619

To my family:
Pilar, Chris, Julian, Lois, and Ree-Ahn

And to all those who, like Katya,
have learned that we really can
trust God—in all things.

Contents

Chapter 1   Goose Girl 9

Chapter 2   The Forbidden Haircut 20

Chapter 3   To Be a Young Pioneer 30

Chapter 4   "Religion Is Dangerous!" 40

Chapter 5   The First Big Competition 50

Chapter 6   Skiing Is More Important Than School 60

Chapter 7   The Team Becomes Everything 70

Chapter 8   The Bible Is Real! 80

Chapter 9   Trying to Serve Two Masters 91

Chapter 10   Everything for Jesus 100

Chapter 11   More Choices 108

Chapter 12   When God Leads .118

Chapter 1

Goose Girl

Watching geese is boring," 9-year-old Katya (COT-cha) muttered to herself as she dangled her bare feet in the river. She enjoyed visiting her father's parents, Baba Katya and Dido Vania (VAN-ya), for the summer, but she hated watching Baba Katya's geese.

The big gray-and-white birds honked gently as they nibbled at the weeds in the meadow beside the river. There was nothing interesting about that. She had been watching these same geese since they were tiny goslings, and she didn't care if she never saw a goose again.

The birds hated her. Especially the leader. He often nipped her with his hard bill, and it hurt. She did not like the geese any more than they liked her.

Katya turned all the way around, looking at the typical late-summer scenery of the Ukraine. Beyond the river, she saw golden wheat fields, meadows, and the village in which her grandparents lived. Off to the right she could see people moving in the fields of the collective farm.

Well, that had not taken long.

She took two small cars out of her pocket and tried to make a road for them in the thick grass, but the cars kept getting caught on the grassy clumps. She couldn't make them go more than a few inches. Besides, it was no fun playing alone. She wished her dog, Hipka, were here. He would put those geese in their place in no time. And he would be someone to play with.

In disgust she shoved the cars back into her pocket.

She threw some stones. She braided stems of rye grass and tied the braid to the end of a stick. Then she dangled the braid in the water, trying to catch a fish. She saw one fish, but it swam right past it without even looking at the braid.

Katya tossed the stick aside. "Stupid geese!" she exclaimed.

The lead gander took offense at her exclamation and ran toward her, hissing, wings outspread. Katya danced out of his way.

"Go back! Get away from me!" she yelled, grabbing the stick again and swinging it as hard as she could. Finally she drove the gander back. Still grumbling, he paced off to the flock, but kept turning to glare and hiss at her.

"Forget these stupid birds," Katya exclaimed. "If Baba Katya wants them watched, she can watch them herself! I'm going to find someone to play with."

Katya rolled down the legs of her trousers and

skipped off toward the village in which her grandparents lived. She told herself she was glad that she had left the geese. They were stupid birds anyway.

But deep down she knew she was wrong. Baba Katya trusted her to watch the geese. What if a fox came and ate one? Or a wolf? A wolf could eat several of them at once. Baba Katya depended on these birds to make the money she needed to buy supplies for the winter.

Katya loved her grandmother. She did not want her to go hungry this winter. Maybe it was wrong to leave. Maybe she—

"Katya!"

Katya spun around when she heard her name. There were Frozina and Annychka, her two friends from the village, running toward her across the grassy steppe.

"Hi, Frozina! Hi, Annychka! What are you doing here? Aren't you supposed to be watching your mothers' geese?"

"Oh, geese!" spat Frozina. "Stupid birds. We left them to watch themselves."

"But—what if something happens to them?" asked Katya.

"Nothing ever happens to them," declared Annychka. "Now, are you going to play with us or not?"

"Yes. Of course I'm going to play." Katya's fears for the geese were relieved by the assurances of her friends.

"What should we play?" asked Frozina. "Shall we play house?"

"No! Let's play cars," urged Katya, pulling all three of her small cars out of her pocket.

"See? I have one for each of us. We can build a road and race them."

Annychka looked around at the grassland. "How can we build a road in this?" she asked.

"We'll go under the bridge at the river. There's lots of dirt under there," Katya told her.

So the girls headed for the wooden bridge. Soon they had smoothed a long "road" and had their cars lined up for the race.

"Ready! Set! Go!" cried Katya, and all three began running, bent over, pushing their cars.

Suddenly, Frozina swerved to her left and ran into Katya. Katya fell sideways, knocking Annychka down with her.

"You did that on purpose!" yelled Katya.

Frozina laughed. "Too bad. You lose," she called back, still running. "I win."

Katya's face turned scarlet as her temper boiled over. Jumping to her feet, she charged.

Frozina blanched when she saw her angry friend lunging toward her. She turned to run, but it was too late. Katya leaped on the other girl, dragging her down, and pounded her with her fists.

"You cheated! You cheated!" screamed Katya.

"Stop! Stop it!" Frozina sobbed, holding her

hands in front of her face to protect it; but Katya didn't stop.

Annychka tugged at Katya's jacket. "Katya," she pleaded. "Stop it. Please stop."

Katya sat up, still straddling Frozina. "Say you're sorry," she ordered.

"I'm—I'm sor-sorry," gulped Frozina.

"All right, then," said Katya, scrambling to her feet. "But don't you ever cheat again," she warned darkly. "Next time I won't let you off so easy."

Frozina nodded. Carefully she picked up her car, and the three children began playing again. The fight was quickly forgotten as they heaped up dirt to make roads. They stuck twigs in the dirt for trees, and piles of grass became houses.

After a while they pretended that the cars were military vehicles from countries at war. They spent quite some time attacking each other's "convoys."

When they tired of that game, they sat beside the road, trying to think of something else to play.

"I know," said Frozina after they'd sat for a while. "We can play campfire."

"Yes!" Campfire was one of Katya's favorite games. But where could they play it?

"There's a big pile of straw behind our house," said Frozina. "We can use some of it."

"Won't your parents be mad?" asked Annychka.

"We'll just use a little. They'll never know," Frozina told her.

But Annychka still wasn't sure. "Come on, Annychka," jeered Katya. "What are you? A sissy? I dare you."

Annychka couldn't turn down a dare, so the three of them hurried to the village and sneaked into Frozina's backyard.

"See? There's the straw," Frozina pointed out.

Quickly the children gathered little piles of straw, then competed to see who could get her straw burning fastest.

"I win!" crowed Katya. "See? There's smoke coming up from it." Sure enough, her pile of straw was smoldering and smoking. Suddenly it burst into flame.

"Yeah! I win, you lose," chanted Katya.

Just then a gust of wind caught the fire, and little tongues of flame darted across the grass.

"Put it out!" screamed Frozina. "You'll burn our house down!"

"We'll burn down the whole village if the fire gets away from us!" shouted Annychka.

At that, all three girls ran around the yard, stamping on every little spark and curl of smoke they could find.

"Frozina!" called a woman's voice. The children froze. Had they been discovered?

"Come to supper," the voice called. Frozina spun around.

"The geese! I have to go get my mother's geese!"

She ran out of the yard and down the road toward the meadow.

"I'd better go too," said Annychka. "My mother must be looking for me." And she was gone as well.

But Katya was the fastest runner in the village—faster even than the boys. She soon passed her two friends as they all ran for the meadow to collect their flocks of geese.

Reaching the spot at the bottom of the hill where she'd left Baba Katya's geese, Katya skidded to a stop. The geese were gone! What would she tell Baba Katya? These birds were Baba Katya's income. What would she say?

With a groan Katya began to trudge along the road back to the village. She tried to think of a convincing story to explain the missing geese. But she could not come up with anything.

As she approached her grandparents' little house, she saw Dido Vania sitting on the porch in the sunshine. He looked angry. But then, he often looked angry. During World War II Dido Vania had suffered an injury to his legs and back. He could not work, and his helplessness made him angry. He complained a lot.

"Naughty girl!" Dido Vania bellowed as soon as he saw her. His deep, angry voice scared her. "You ran off and left your grandmother's geese alone." He shook his fist. "How do you think we will live through the winter if we don't have the money the geese bring in?"

Katya's heart sank. The geese were dead. A wolf or a fox had gotten into the flock and killed them. All because she had run away to play. She hung her head.

"They might have been killed!" roared Dido Vania.

Katya's head snapped up. "They aren't dead?" she squeaked.

"No, but they well could be," rumbled Dido Vania. "They came home by themselves a few minutes ago. Your grandmother is very angry with you, young lady. Go out back and see what she has to say."

"Yes, Dido Vania," Katya murmured as she scurried out of his reach.

Baba Katya was in the backyard, fastening the goose pen. The big birds honked softly as they settled down for the evening.

Baba Katya turned a furious face to her granddaughter. "You left my geese alone. How could you be so naughty?"

Once again Katya hung her head. "But, Baba Katya, they're all right, aren't they?"

"No thanks to you, you naughty girl. They could have been killed on the road. Or a wolf could have eaten them."

Suddenly Baba Katya's anger seemed to evaporate. "Call Dido Vania for supper," she said evenly. Then she turned around and marched into the house.

After supper Baba Katya came to Katya's room carrying a big knife and two bags. "Come, Katya.

We're going to work in the garden," she said, handing her one of the bags.

Together the old woman and the young girl walked down the dirt road, out of the village, and to the family garden plot.

The sunflowers were full of ripe seeds. The heavy heads hung low. Baba Katya grabbed a flower head and cut through the thick stem with the knife. She handed the flower head to Katya, who stuffed it into one of the bags. As they worked, Baba Katya began to tell a story.

"In the 1930s, when I was a young woman, Stalin decided to wipe out religion. You know who Stalin was, don't you?"

"He was the second great premier of the glorious Soviet Union," Katya answered, quoting her teachers. Baba Katya grunted but did not comment. She continued her story.

"Many people were scared, so they gave in and got rid of their Bibles. Others hid their Bibles. Sometimes people working for the state came to the houses and searched for Bibles. If a Bible was found in a home, that family had to pay a fine.

"Some of the people who searched the houses did not believe in God. Others were just scared, so they tried to look as though they were good Communists and atheists."

"What did they do with the Bibles?" asked Katya.

"They collected all the Bibles they could find," said Baba Katya. "Eventually they carried them all to the park. There they piled up the Bibles and danced on them."

Baba Katya shook her head.

"That was a very bad thing to do," she said. "That was blasphemy. But the people were more afraid of the state than they were of God. After they danced on the holy books, they set them afire and burned them. Oh, what an evil thing to do!" Baba Katya was nearly weeping now. "They took our family Bible with the names and dates of marriages, births, and deaths written in it. It was our family record, but it is gone forever."

Katya reached out and patted her grandmother's hand. "I'm very sorry, Baba Katya."

The old woman tried to smile. "Don't be sorry for me, Katya. Be sorry for the unfaithful ones who treated the Bible with blasphemy."

"Why? What happened to them?" asked Katya.

Baba Katya looked off in the distance, the light of the sinking sun brightening her wrinkled face.

"I remember one family," she said. "They thought they were safe because they collected many Bibles and burned them. It was a big family—lots of sons, cousins, and uncles. Just a few months after the Bible-burning, one of the sons drowned in this very river that flows past our village."

Katya shivered as she looked toward the river. It did not look dangerous now, but she knew that in the spring it sometimes flooded and was full of fast currents and eddies.

"Then," Baba Katya continued, "one of the cousins was hit by a car and killed. And an uncle walked past a wall just as it fell, and it killed him."

By this time Katya's mouth was hanging open. So many horrible things to happen to one family!

"Another son died of a terrible fever," said Baba Katya. She turned and looked at Katya, her dark eyes flashing golden sparks in the last rays of sunlight.

"So you see, Katya, it does not pay to reject God. It does not pay to blaspheme."

Katya stared.

"Never reject God," Baba Katya said firmly. "Never."

"I won't," Katya promised, shaking her head vigorously. "And I'll never blaspheme." *Even when I find out what that means,* she thought.

Baba Katya patted the girl's shoulder. "That's good. Because God punishes those who reject Him. Now, let us go home. It is almost dark." Each slung a heavy sack of sunflower heads over her shoulder, and they started home.

It was spooky, walking along the road in the shadowy dusk. Now and then Katya heard a rustling in the grass or felt a sudden breeze, and she had to force herself not to whimper. She was safe, she told herself. God would not punish her. She did not reject Him. She was not a blasphemer.

Nevertheless, she reached out and took hold of Baba Katya's hand.

Chapter 2

The Forbidden Haircut

One day, near the end of Katya's visit, her babushka (Ba-BOOSH-ka; it means "grandmother") decided to slaughter some geese. This was a chance for Katya to make up for her earlier misbehavior. Katya enjoyed helping Baba with everything. Happily she trotted out to the backyard to where Baba Katya was waiting near the goose pen.

"Grab that one." Baba Katya indicated a fat gray goose, and Katya caught it by one leg. The goose squawked, and Katya jerked her head back to avoid being slapped in the face by the bird's powerful wings.

As Katya pushed down the goose's neck across the old stump that served as a cutting block, Baba Katya grabbed the bird's head and lowered the sharp butcher knife. She was going to saw the neck in two.

Suddenly Katya could not stand to watch. For the first time, it seemed cruel, and she turned and ran to the house. Baba Katya's laughter followed her. Katya slammed the door and ran clear through the house to the parlor, where she hunkered down on the floor behind the couch. She did not come out until she heard her grandmother come into the kitchen.

"I will help you clean the goose, Baba Katya," the girl said meekly.

"Good. Don't worry about your weak stomach," said Baba Katya kindly. "You're just like your mama—tenderhearted." She shook her head. "Not good for a farm girl, but I suppose you have other plans for your life."

"I don't have any plans right now," Katya admitted, "except to join the Pioneers this coming school year."

"You have to be a very good girl for that," Baba Katya reminded her.

"I know. I will be good. I will," Katya insisted.

And she tried very hard to be good. She did not want to make Baba Katya and Dido Vania feel bad. And she did not want to get yelled at either, especially by Dido Vania, with his deep, scary voice.

But the whole world seemed to conspire against her. The remaining geese continued to torment her, she was bored, and the weather was hot. One afternoon a few days later she sat beside the stream and pushed her long, heavy hair away from her neck and back. For just a moment the breeze cooled her sweaty skin.

"You should have your baba cut your hair. Mine did," said a voice behind her.

Katya whirled around to find Frozina standing behind her, grinning. Frozina's golden-blond hair had been cut into a smooth oval around her face.

"Oh, Frozina! Your hair is lovely," exclaimed Katya.

"It's a lot cooler this way, too," Frozina said. "You really should get your baba to cut yours."

Katya ran her fingers through her thick hair. It reached below her waist. Baba Katya and Dido Vania liked her long hair. They called it her crowning glory.

A crowning glory may be fine in winter, thought Katya, *but in summer it is just too hot.* The more she thought about cutting her hair, the more excited she got. She could hardly wait to get back to the house in the evening.

As soon as she ran into the kitchen, she asked, "Baba Katya, will you cut my hair? It's so hot. Short hair would be much more comfortable."

"Cut your beautiful hair? Absolutely not!" answered Baba Katya, shocked.

"Don't even think about it," ordered Dido Vania.

Katya did not say anything, but she pouted through supper and chores. As soon as possible, she mumbled a sulky "Good night" to her grandparents and went off to her bedroom. Ukrainian houses were big, and Baba and Dido had had five children, so they had several bedrooms. Katya's room was far away from that of her grandparents.

Suddenly she had a brilliant thought. If she waited until her grandparents were asleep, they would not hear her leave her room. She could cut her hair then, and they would not wake up. Once it was done, what could they say?

Baba Katya worked until late, as she did every

night. Katya found it hard to stay awake while she waited. But at last the house was quiet. Katya waited a little longer to be sure her grandparents were asleep. Then she stole quietly out of her room and made her way stealthily to the living room. She fumbled in Baba Katya's sewing basket and found the scissors. She did not dare turn on a light. She just held her hair at the length she thought it should be, and she snipped. She snipped and snipped.

She felt all over her head with one hand while with the other she cut her hair into what she was sure was the same style as Frozina's.

Oh, yes! With her hair shoulder-length, her back was a lot cooler, and it was easier to lift the hair from her neck to catch a cooling breeze. Now she would be able to sleep comfortably. Still working by feel, she swept up the hair from the floor and tossed it into a wastebasket. Then she tiptoed back to her room and crawled into bed. She was soon sound asleep.

It seemed no time before the crowing of the village roosters awoke Katya. They must be wrong. It could not be time to get up already. But when she opened her eyes, she saw that the sky was indeed light at the horizon.

"Time to get up, lazybones," came Baba Katya's cheerful voice outside the bedroom door.

Katya scrambled out of bed, forgetting all about her haircut. Quickly she dressed and hurried to the kitchen to help her grandmother get breakfast.

Baba Katya was cracking eggs into a bowl when she caught sight of Katya in the doorway. Her mouth fell open.

"Katya!" she gasped. "What have you done to your hair?"

Suddenly Katya remembered, and her hand went to her hair. "It was just too hot the other way," she argued. "I had to cut it."

"Have you *seen* yourself?" asked Baba Katya. The girl shook her head. "Come here." Baba Katya led her granddaughter into the living room and stood her in front of the mirror.

Horrors! Instead of lying neatly in the smooth, oval style Katya had imagined, her hair stuck out all over her head. Worse, it seemed that no two strands were the same length. She looked like a crooked pincushion.

"Baba Katya," she wailed. "Please fix my hair. You can make it all even."

But the woman shook her head. "Not a hair will I touch."

"Then I'll go to the hairdresser. She will make it all right," Katya said hopefully.

Baba Katya shook her head again.

"You disobeyed. You were determined to have short hair no matter what we said. Now that you have it, you can just live with it. Let's see what your parents say when their little porcupine comes home."

And before Katya could get used to her awful

hair, it was time to return home. Dido Vania came home with Alexander Govorov (GO-vor-off) and his wife, Olga Govorovna (GO-vor-OHV-na), who were friends of Katya's parents back home in Karamken. They had brought her to the Ukraine with them, and they would accompany her home.

"Hello, Uncle. Hello, Aunt," said Katya politely, in the way Russian children addressed adults.

"Hello, Katya," said Uncle Alexander and Aunt Olga. They kept looking at her hair, and Katya wished she could wear a stocking cap to hide it. But this was summer, and any cap was too hot. She looked down at the floor.

"Katya," said Aunt Olga, "who cut your hair? I've never seen quite that look before."

"I cut it," mumbled Katya, her face red with embarrassment.

"Oh," said Aunt Olga. After that, she did not refer to Katya's hair again.

Baba Katya and Dido Vania hugged Katya goodbye. Then she picked up her bags and followed Uncle and Aunt out into the road.

The road led down the hill to the river at the bottom. Katya looked around to the meadow where she had herded the geese. They had all been slaughtered or sold by now. They would not torment her anymore this year.

Thinking about that made Katya feel better. She lifted her head. She really did feel cooler with short hair. She began to smile.

Within minutes the three had reached the bus stop beside the river. When the bus came by, Uncle Alexander flagged it down. The driver stepped down and opened the baggage compartment so they could stow their belongings. Then they all climbed up into the bus, Uncle paid the driver, and they were on their way.

As Katya sat looking out the window of the bus, thinking about the long journey home, she sensed someone looking at her. She looked up to see the man in the seat ahead, twisted around and staring at her. "Little girl," said the man, "who cut your hair?"

Katya ducked her head. "I did, Uncle," she replied.

"Oh," said the man. "I thought it might be something like that."

Although he had been polite and had not made fun of her, Katya was ashamed. It was several minutes before she looked up again.

After an hour's ride, the bus stopped at a train station. Katya was glad to get out of the bus. As they waited on the platform for the train to come, she tried not to catch anyone's eye.

But when the train arrived, the conductor looked closely at her. As she stepped up into the train, he asked the question she knew was coming. "Who cut your hair, little girl?"

And again she had to admit that she had done it.

Oh, how she wished she had obeyed!

There was nobody else in the train compartment with her and her escorts, and Katya was glad of that. For a while she could relax and not wait for someone to ask the Question.

At suppertime Katya opened the basket of food that Baba Katya had sent with her. Baba Katya had packed several kinds of *varenyky*. These were little pockets made of boiled dough and filled with such good things as potato and cheese, sauerkraut, or cottage cheese. Some even had blueberries or cherries inside.

Baba Katya had also included several apples and fresh peaches, as well as some sweet cherries wrapped up in a napkin. For dessert there were some *khrustyky*, sweet, deep-fried pastry flavored with almonds. And of course there were lots of roasted and salted sunflower seeds for snacks.

They slept on the train, and in the morning they arrived in Moscow. From there they would take a plane across Russia to the city of Magadan (MAH-gah-dahn), main city of the Kolyma (KOHL-ih-ma) region, far away, east of Siberia.

When they got aboard the plane, Katya had to sit in a row in front of Uncle's and Aunt's seats. When the woman seated next to her looked at her intently, Katya scooted down in her seat, but she knew she could not avoid the Question.

"Little girl, who cut your hair?" asked the woman.

Katya was ready to scream.

For the next eight hours she sat very still in her seat. Now and then someone would walk past, take a second look, and ask about her hair. Finally Katya pretended to be asleep.

In Magadan they got on another bus, and two hours later they were finally at Karamken. The settlement's name meant "windy" in the language of the Chuckcha people, who were the original inhabitants. And the place lived up to its name.

Mama met the train. She smiled when she saw Katya step down from the bus, but her smile quickly faded when she saw that her hair was not merely windblown.

"Katya!" exclaimed Mama. "What happened to your hair?"

Katya hung her head. "I'm sorry, Mama." Then her words came in a rush. "It was so hot, just so hot, every day. I couldn't stand it, Mama, so I *had* to cut it. You understand, don't you? You'll let me go to the hairdresser, won't you? The hairdresser can fix it."

"Why did you cut your own hair, Katya?" asked Mama sternly. "Why didn't Baba Katya cut it?"

Katya's heart beat hard, and she looked at the ground.

Katya's words were barely audible. "She said no."

Mama shook her head but did not say anything more. When they got home, Katya had to explain all over again to Papa.

"I can go to the hairdresser, can't I, Papa?" begged

Katya, even though she knew that Papa hated to spend money.

"You got your wish for short hair. That is enough," Papa declared. "You will not go to the hairdresser. You will wear your hair just as it is until it grows out. We'll see how soon you disobey again." He picked up his paper and began to read.

Katya was close to tears, but she did not dare argue with Papa. Hipka whined in sympathy and licked her hand, but it did not help. She would have to go to school with her chopped-up hair. And for months, until it grew out again, she would have to endure the teasing of her classmates.

As usual, winter came early to the tundra. With the numerous other children of Karamken settlement, Katya often went cross-country skiing, when they weren't ice skating on the frozen Kolyma River or digging caves in the snow.

But she walked to school because she had to cross a busy highway that was not friendly to skiers. The walk was not long—only about five minutes—but she was glad that a warm woolen hat covered her head. In addition to wanting protection from the cold, she did not want the other children to tease her about her hair.

The way to school led through dilapidated garages and a factory that dated from the Stalin era, which had ended more than 20 years ago. When Katya was younger, she and her friends had searched through the rubble for old journals, books, and other items from the factory. They used these rescued treasures to play office or school. But the factory always made Katya shiver a little.

The factory had been part of the slave-labor camps

Stalin had built. Political prisoners had been sent way out here, where there was no point in escaping the camp because there was no place to go. Then they were put to work building roads, digging in the gold mines, or laboring in the factories to process the ore.

After Stalin's death, the government closed the camps. To attract young families to build up settlements in the area, the government paid high wages. In a sort of gold rush, young people came from all over Russia to find their fortunes in the frozen east.

Katya's father and mother were two who had come. They hoped to save enough money to buy a big house in central Russia.

Papa had told her about his early days in the Kolyma region, when he worked at setting up utility poles along the slave-built road from Magadan, the capital, into the far north of the region.

"Every once in a while, when we were digging holes to set the poles in, we would find a skull. Each skull had a bullet hole in the forehead," said Papa.

"How did that happen?" Katya had asked, her eyes wide.

"If a prisoner became too ill or too weak to work, he was shot and buried beside the road."

The factory always reminded Katya of her father's story, and whenever she had to pass it, she hurried a little faster.

Katya's family lived in one of the many barracks that had been used to house the prisoners. Four families lived in each barracks, with a separate entrance for each family. Katya and her parents had one small room, a tiny corridor and a kitchenette. The wooden outdoor toilet, about 10 yards from the barracks, was unheated.

One morning, when Katya opened the outside door, she saw a wall of snow blocking the doorway. This often happened in winter, and it was her job to shovel the snow away. Sighing, she picked up the shovel from the corner.

The snow came about halfway up the house, and then a drift curved up to the roof. As Katya plunged the shovel into the drift, it collapsed, sending a shower of snow into the corridor around her. She began to toss shovelfuls of flakes up over the remaining snow.

When she had cleared a small space directly in front of the door, she stood on that spot and began to clear out a step a little higher than where she now stood. She continued in this way until she had dug a series of steps up from the corridor to the top of the solid snow cover. It was almost like a tunnel, with snow on both sides of the steps.

By the time she was finished, she had to hurry to get to school on time. She reached the schoolyard with only minutes to spare. Just as she was crossing the playground, a snowball slammed into her face. The snowball had ice in the middle, and it hurt. Clapping her mittened hand to her stinging cheek, Katya looked around.

Boris, a boy in her grade, stood grinning at her.

Katya had been trying hard to stay out of fights so she could be inducted into the Pioneers, but this was too much. She flew at Boris in a fury, pounding him with her fists and feet. The other students stood around, watching.

"Help!" yelled Boris. "Get her off me!" But nobody moved. They knew how well Katya could fight, and they were not taking any chances of getting her mad at them.

Suddenly Katya felt a jerk on her collar as someone yanked her off Boris. At first she struggled, but then she heard the stern voice of Galina Stepanovna, her teacher.

"Katya! Stop it!" Katya instantly went limp, and Stepanovna dropped her. "You will stay after school today," the teacher commanded. "Your parents will be called. Now go to class."

That was a miserable day. Hour after hour Katya found it impossible to pay attention to class. All she could think about was facing her parents after school.

Finally the dreaded moment arrived. The other children had gone when Katya's parents arrived. She sat at her desk, avoiding their eyes, as Mama and Papa took seats to one side of the teacher.

"What are we going to do with you, Katya?" asked the teacher. "Well?" she prompted when Katya failed to respond.

"I don't know, Galina Stepnanovna," whispered Katya.

"This is the second time this week that I have had to call your parents to my office because of your misbehavior. And three times last week. And twice the week before. Every week your parents come to see me. I am getting to know them better than my own family."

"But Boris—"

"Boris is being punished," said Stepanovna. "I know he was naughty. But your response was way out of line. Do you even realize how hard you hit and kicked him?" Katya shook her head. "If you had stuck a vital organ, you could have caused him grave damage."

"I'm sorry," murmured Katya.

"You are always sorry," said Stepanovna, her voice hard. "You have shamed your parents. I will leave it to them to punish you."

Katya began to tremble. She knew what the punishment would be.

Sure enough, as soon as they arrived home, she saw Papa taking off his belt. "Katya," he said sternly, "take off your coat and lie on your couch."

Fighting back tears, Katya went to the corner where her folding couch stood. She removed her coat and lay down on her stomach. She heard the belt whistle through the air just before she felt its sting. She braced herself, but she still jumped. She couldn't help it. It hurt so badly!

Again and again the belt lashed her body. At last Mama gasped, "Anatoly, surely that's enough."

But Papa snapped the belt in her direction, and

Katya heard Mama's yelp through the pounding in her own ears.

"I will say when it is enough, Tamara," Papa shouted, his face red with anger. Finally, he stopped, panting from his exertion. "Go to bed," he ordered.

Doing her best to stifle her sobs, Katya stood up, slowly unfolded the couch, and made up her bed. On the other side of the room, Mama was crying softly. Katya carefully got into bed. She hurt. She hurt so much.

Why does Papa have to be so mean? she wondered. She wished she had a papa who was kind to her. One who would make her feel that he actually wanted her.

But by the next day at school Katya was able to put the beating to the back of her mind in her excitement over the Young Pioneers. The children in her grade buzzed with eagerness as they stood in front of the pictures of Vladimir Lenin and Josef Stalin that hung in the school's entry.

Lenin, especially, was revered as the leader of the Bolsheviks, who, during the 1917 Russian Revolution, had seized control of the tsarist government. He was the first premier of the Soviet Union. Stalin had succeeded to the premiership after Lenin's death.

Both men had been viciously cruel, but now that aspect was downplayed, and they were admired for their leadership of the country. Stalin had had been denounced by Premier Nikita Khrushchev in 1956, but a mystical, almost golden, aura still surrounded his name.

The children had been taught to consider both men heroes. Now they stared worshipfully at the photos of these two legendary leaders. Everyone was murmuring the word "Pioneers." This was the day the lists would come out.

The Young Pioneers was somewhat similar to Boy Scouts and Girl Scouts. But it was the second of three organizations set up to train children to become good citizens of the Communist Party. At age 7 Katya and all of her classmates had joined the first organization, the Oktyabryata (OK-tee-ah-BREE-ah-tah, or Little Octoberists, a reference to the Russian Revolution).

Membership in both these organizations was required in the U.S.S.R., but more was demanded of Young Pioneers. Each Pioneer would have the responsibility of teaching good citizenship to a cell of five Little Octoberists. Therefore, children had to be on their best behavior in order to be inducted into the Pioneers.

Each Pioneer proudly wore a pin with a red star. In the center of the star was a picture of Lenin as a child. Wearing the pin was a source of pride. The pin meant the child was part of the community. Everybody had one. But since induction was a sign of good citizenship and acceptance, a child who misbehaved would be humiliated by having to wait for the second ceremony a month later.

The third step was the All-Union Leninist

Communist Union of Youth, better known as the Komsomol (COMB-so-mole). Although this organization was not mandatory, almost everyone joined about age 14. In fact, only members, or Komsomolets (COMB-so-MOE-lots), had a chance to go to college and find a good career.

Just then the children saw Galina Stepanovna come out of her office with the lists in her hands. Taking her time, she taped the lists to the walls. As soon as her office door closed behind her, the children surged forward to look for their names.

Breathlessly Katya scanned the first page, then the second. With a sinking feeling in the pit of her stomach, she carefully read each name on the third page. Then she went back and slowly read the first two pages. Her name was not there.

As one after another of the other children found their own names on the lists they shouted and shrieked with excitement. Katya hoped they didn't notice her silence. She drifted backward, out of the crowd, and then turned away. Hurrying to the restroom, she hid in a stall until the bell rang for class.

Back with the other students, she tried to smile and act as though everything was all right. She saw several boys looking positively glum. Boris was one of them. So he was not getting a Young Pioneer scarf either! Somehow, it made her feel worse to know that she was grouped with him and his buddies. They were *really* bad. She was only a little bit bad.

The night of the induction ceremony came. Katya did not want to go, but all the students were required to be there. She sat in the assembly room with her mother, trying to make herself invisible. She watched as the happy children from her class filed onto the platform and stood facing the audience. Their faces glowed with pride.

The contrast between them and her made Katya even more ashamed. Everyone in the settlement knew how bad Boris and his friends were. Almost everyone had had trouble with those boys. *Now,* Katya thought, *people will think I'm just like them.*

Galina Stepanovna gave a speech about the glories of Communism, but Katya hardly heard a word. She was trying too hard not to cry. The golden moment had turned to ashes. The humiliation was almost more than she could bear.

The band struck up the national anthem, and the audience rose to their feet. A Pioneer stepped up to each inductee, removed the Oktyabryenok pin, and replaced it with the red Pioneer scarf, tying the scarf precisely in a special way.

From now on, the new Young Pioneers would wear their red scarves to school every day. They had proven themselves good enough. They belonged.

Everyone cheered and clapped. Tears ran down the cheeks of proud parents all over the room. Katya stole a glance at Mama. She was applauding the children on stage. She did not look at Katya or say anything to hurt her. Nevertheless, Katya felt the weight of her mother's disappointment.

As soon as the ceremony was over, Katya slipped away from her mother and hid in the girls' restroom until it was time to leave. She did not want anyone to see her without a red scarf.

For the next several weeks, whenever she was not in class, Katya hid in the restroom. She did not get into any trouble. How could she? Hidden away in the restroom stall, she could not get into fights with anybody.

Finally the second Pioneers ceremony was held. It was smaller, and there were fewer cheers and less applause. Mama smiled at her from the audience, but somehow it was not the same. It was only second-best.

Katya did not really belong.

Sitting at her desk, Katya looked at the funny picture in her history book. It showed a man holding a big stick over his donkey. He was obviously about to strike the animal. The donkey had its mouth open and its head turned toward the man. Under the picture were the words: "One of the many myths of the Bible. This is a fable about a man with a talking donkey."

The children laughed when they saw the page.

Grigori raised his hand. "Galina Stepanovna, is there anything true about the Bible?"

"Of course not," scoffed Luda without even raising her hand. "Religion is the drug of the masses," she recited.

"Good. That is very good, Luda," said Galina Stepanovna. "I am glad to see that you have learned that lesson. As we all know, there is no God. God is just a made-up story, like the rest of these Bible myths. The priests used the myth of God for many years to keep the workers from rising up and breaking their bonds.

"This so-called God did not help the workers when

they were struggling under the burdens that the tsars and the landowners laid on their shoulders, did He?"

The children shook their heads. "No-o," they singsonged in unison.

"Right," said the teacher. "Who did free the workers?"

"The Communist Party freed the workers," chanted the children.

"And remember that religion is not just false. It is dangerous. It is much worse than a drug," she warned.

The children became particularly attentive. Most of them had heard about religion, and some of them, such as Katya, even had religious grandparents. But none of them knew much about religious beliefs.

"All religions are just cults. Of course, there are some depraved people who refuse to accept that there is no God. They make up a God, and then they engage in filthy practices," the teacher continued solemnly. "Sometimes they steal children."

The students gasped in horror.

"It is true. I am sorry to frighten you," she continued, "but I must tell you these things for your own good so that you will know how to protect yourselves." She did not say what happened to those stolen children, but left it to the students' vivid imaginations.

Then she dismissed the class.

As Katya left the school she was thoughtful. The teacher was right, of course. Katya would not think of questioning her. But then, where did that leave Baba

Katya? Baba Katya was not bad, and she believed in God. In fact, she believed that God would punish unbelievers such as Galina Stepanovna.

Katya's head began to spin. She did not know what to think. She was saved from wracking her brain over the problem any longer when Marina and Luda called to her.

"Katya, Katya!" shouted her friends, running to catch up with her. Katya stopped and waited for them.

"Let's go to the cemetery and look at the pictures of the people buried there," Marina suggested.

"All right," said Katya. "Let's go home first, though, and then we can ski to the cemetery."

So the girls hurried home and strapped on their cross-country skis. They met and headed for the cemetery.

"Wasn't that horrible, what Galina Stepanovna said this afternoon?" Marina asked. "Have you ever heard of such terrible things?"

"Never!" Luda cried.

"Actually, I have," said Katya. "Do you remember my Baba Masha, who used to live in Karamken?"

"H'mm. I think so," mused Luda. "Your mother's mother, isn't she? She used to babysit you. Yes, I remember her. Whatever happened to her, anyway?"

"She moved away to central Russia, to the Tambov region."

"Oh. She was so old, I thought she might have died," offered Marina.

"She isn't as old as she looks," Katya told her. "She's had a hard life. But she did almost die. She was almost killed a couple of times."

The other girls' eyes grew large. "Tell us about it," they demanded.

"Well, one time there was a famine, and—"

"The Communist Party has solved the problem of famines. All Russians now have enough to eat," chanted loyal Luda.

"Yes, well, this happened before that. Someone tried to kill her to eat her."

"No!" Katya's friends were horrified.

"Yes, but that's not what I wanted to tell you about. One time she became interested in religion—"

"Ooooh! That was a bad idea," Luda broke in. "Not only was it dangerous, but it was disloyal to the revolution."

"Be quiet, Luda. Let her tell the story," Marina ordered.

"Well, she soon learned her lesson," said Katya quickly, wanting to stop the criticism of her dear babushka.

"She attended meetings of a sect for a while, and she had an experience similar to what Galina Stepanovna told us about."

"What happened?" asked Marina eagerly.

"Well, they were some kind of cult."

"All religions are cults," recited Luda.

"Anyway, these people tried to kill her as a sacrifice," said Katya. "She barely escaped with her life."

Marina's mouth made a big O. "That's even worse than the things Galina Stepanovna was saying."

"I know," said Katya. "It scares me."

"Me too," said Luda. "I'm glad I'm loyal to Lenin and the Russian Revolution. I will never fool around with religion." She shook her head. "I don't have time, anyway. I have to learn the history and principles of the Communist Party so I can join the Komsomol. Maybe we can all study together," she suggested.

"Sure," said Marina.

"Maybe," said Katya, her mind elsewhere.

"Don't you want to be a member of the Komsomol?" demanded Luda.

"Of course," exclaimed Katya, shocked. "I want to go to the university, and I want to get a good job. That's impossible without becoming a Komsomol member."

"But Oktyabryata and Pioneers are compulsory. The Komsomol isn't," Marina warned with a sideways look. "You have to know a lot, and your behavior must bring honor to the party."

Katya's face burned. She knew her friend was referring to her postponed Pioneer ceremony. She knew that her behavior must improve, but, no matter how hard she tried, she just could not make herself good.

The girls walked in silence the last few yards to the cemetery.

Inside they saw row after row of large stone red stars

of the revolution marking the graves. Many relatives had put pictures of their loved ones on the stars. The girls ran around, reading the markers.

"Oh, look at this one," exclaimed Marina. "The marker says that he was a good Communist, faithful to Lenin and Stalin and the revolution. He died in World War II.

"'He lives on in the glorious accomplishments of the Communist Party,'" she read thoughtfully.

"My Baba Katya says that in the old days graves were marked with crosses," observed Katya. She looked out of the corner of her eye to see how Luda would take her remark.

"Yes, back in the days when the priests kept the people drugged by religion," said Luda scornfully.

"The Orthodox churches are topped with gold crosses, even today," said Marina.

"I think the red star looks much better. Don't you?" Luda challenged, running her hand across the point of a star monument.

"Certainly," said Marina.

"Uh, yes, of course," Katya added. "The red star is much better. It commemorates true sacrifice and honorable struggle."

It was the right answer. Luda cheered up and changed the subject.

"Katya, are you going to join the cross-country skiing club?" she asked.

Katya bent down to examine another oval photo

covered in hard plastic. This soldier had been young and handsome. "Are you?" she asked.

"Yes!" Luda was enthusiastic.

"So am I," put in Marina. "It's close to the school. And isn't the coach a friend of your father's, Katya?"

"Yes, Yuri Mikhailevich and my father have been friends for a long time. Still . . ." She let the word drag off into silence. Would it make her life better or worse if she joined a club run by her father's friend?

"Oh, come on. You ski so well."

Marina added the clincher. "All of our classmates are joining. You don't want to be left out, do you?"

"All right," said Katya. "I suppose I might as well join. There's not much else to do, anyway. I sure don't want wrestling or ballet."

And that is how Katya found herself at the next meeting of the ski club. The children's equipment was supplied by the club, and Yuri Mikhailevich made sure that Katya was issued the best available. None of the equipment was great, but Katya's was the newest—or perhaps it would be better to say the least old.

She waxed her skis thoroughly, in the way Papa had taught her, and they slid swiftly across the snow.

Yuri Mikhailevich stood watching the skiers and calling out instructions.

"Lower your arms, Grigori—you're bobbing. That's better."

"Luda! Lean farther forward, and loosen your stance."

"Don't worry, Alexei, falling is normal. Just get up and go again."

"Katya, move your arms from the shoulders, not the elbows. The muscles in your back and shoulders are stronger than the ones in your arms. Let the big muscles do most of the work."

Katya's cross-country technique quickly improved, and with it her enjoyment of skiing. She found that she was very fast on the flat terrain. When the children progressed to short races, Katya enjoyed it even more because she was usually the winner, beating even the boys. It was fun to be skiing with her classmates. She was glad she had joined the club.

Then one day when she came home from school the sun shone warm and golden, and she saw puddles of snowmelt all through the town.

When she reached the old barracks, she could hear Hipka whining from his place in the tiny corridor. Hurriedly she opened the door, and Hipka shot outside, shaking himself and spraying water as he ran.

Since the snow was piled above the house, the water now ran downhill, under the door and into the corridor. Automatically Katya went to the kitchen and found a metal bowl. With this she bailed water, tossing it out to one side of the door until it sank into the soft snow.

There would be no school tomorrow. The whole settlement would be flooded. Spring had come to the tundra.

Spring and summer were a trying time for Katya. Papa's temper did not improve, no matter how much money they made from the family's greenhouse. Too many times Katya felt the lash of his leather belt. She longed to get away. Why couldn't she have a loving family?

When school started again, Katya was happy to be able to leave home for the whole day, but unfortunately she continued to get into fights. That meant punishment, both at school and at home. No matter how hard she tried, she just could not make herself be good.

The next winter the ski club moved to the far end of town. Katya had to walk a long way to the meetings. She would stop on the way at Luda's house, and the two of them would walk together. Eventually Katya found her interest waning, in spite of the racing.

One afternoon, when she reached Luda's house, her friend was not ready.

"Just a few minutes," Luda called. "I've been playing with my doll, and I have to put it away."

Katya's ears pricked up. "Doll?"

"Yes. I know that 11 is a little old for dolls, but my babushka just sent me a new one, and I like to play with her. Would you like to see her?"

"Yes!" Katya had spent the first few years of her life wearing boys' clothes and playing boys' games. Just recently she had discovered her girlish side, and she played with dolls almost frantically. Mama joked that Katya was trying to make up for lost time.

Katya dropped her skis outside the door, and soon the two girls were so absorbed in their play that they forgot all about the time. After a long while Katya happened to look up, and when she saw the clock, she froze.

"Luda!" she gasped in fright, jumping to her feet. "Look at the time. We've missed the ski club meeting. Papa will *kill* me!"

Luda grabbed Katya's arm as Katya hurried to leave. "Sit back down. If you wait 20 more minutes, the ski meeting will be out. You can go home then, and your father will never know you missed the meeting."

Katya slowly sat back down. She hoped Luda was right.

When Katya got home, she began to carefully clean and wax her skis as though she had been running on them for the last two hours.

"How did the ski club meeting go, Katya?" asked Papa.

"Oh, it was fine," said Katya, trying to sound enthusiastic.

"Did you win any races?" asked Mama.

"Yes, I won every race I entered. It was funny to see the looks on the boys' faces when I beat them." Katya laughed, and so did her parents.

Katya's heart was beating hard. She hoped that her answers would satisfy her parents. Evidently the answers were good enough, for Mama and Papa returned to their reading and left her alone. As soon as she could, Katya crawled into bed and pretended to be asleep.

She was safe!

After that, she often skipped club meetings to play with Luda. Papa never noticed, and Katya forgot to be afraid.

And then one night when she returned home, Papa was waiting with his belt in his hand.

Katya's heart dropped into the pit of her stomach.

"I saw Yuri Mikhailevich today," said Papa. "He told me that he was sorry you didn't enjoy the ski club enough to come to all the meetings."

Katya hung her head. Her throat was so dry she could not have spoken if her life had depended upon it. At Papa's command she walked silently to her bed in the corner and lay down on her stomach.

It was the worst beating Papa had ever given her. He used the buckle end of the belt this time. When he finally stopped, she pressed her face into the pillow to stifle her sobs and muttered, "I hate Papa!"

It would take a long time for the bruises to heal.

She was glad when summer came, for then she could go to training camp. That summer Katya's training coach was Dimitri Vasilevich.

Of course, there was no way to use ordinary skis in the summertime. The children lined up in front of the coach's cabin, eager to see what he had planned. The door opened, and Dimitri Vasilevich stepped out, carrying some strange-looking contraptions that appeared to be skis with wheels.

"Wheels, Coach?" questioned the children.

"Wheels," he confirmed. "You will run along the roads on these so that you can stay in condition for competition. These take less effort, though, and if you let your legs get lazy, you will not be able to set the wax of your snow skis in the snow. You must be sure to ski on these roller skis just as you would on snow skis, with a quick, downward punch."

Along with the other campers, Katya hurried to strap on her new roller skis. Positioning her poles, she pushed off. Coach Vasilevich was right; this was easier than snow skiing. She followed his advice and gave the roller skis the same strong kick she always gave her snow skis.

Out on the road flowed the students, following the coach. The camp terrain was a little rougher than the nearly flat land at home.

"You have to learn to go uphill and downhill," the coach explained as they rolled along. "Most cross-country competition includes at least some hills."

Not all of Katya's classmates were at the camp. Some were not interested in competitive skiing. Katya felt sorry for them. They did not know what fun they were missing.

They had to stay home and study Soviet history so they could become Komsomol members and have a good career. But Katya was certain there was no better career than skiing.

The children who attended the camp went through three training sessions a day, six days a week, rolling for many kilometers along the roads.

Of course, it was not all work. In the evenings the campers enjoyed scaring each other with ghost stories. They seemed to have an inexhaustible supply of them. And they played pranks on one another. One night they slathered toothpaste on the faces of sleeping teammates. Other times they hid teammates' clothes. The victims were angry at first, but soon they joined in the laughter—and got even by playing pranks of their own. Katya got her share of toothpaste in the face.

Then one evening Katya approached a girl named Svetlana.

"Sveta, you have such beautiful hair," she said. "Where did you get your permanent?"

Sveta tossed her shining, beautifully curled hair. "I got it at the hairdresser's in town. I'll take you there, if you want."

"Oh, yes! Please do!" said Katya eagerly.

So the next time the campers went to town, Sveta took her to the hairdresser's.

"Fix her hair just like mine," Sveta told the woman who ran the shop. Katya sat nervously in the chair and tried to be still as the hairdresser washed, rolled, and treated her hair. It was hard to wait, and oh, those chemicals smelled terrible.

Katya clutched the towel that kept her hair and the chemicals back off her face. "Is it time yet?" she asked. "Can we rinse it off?"

"Wel-l-l," answered the hairdresser slowly, "I guess it depends on how much curl you want."

"Oh, I want lots of curl," said Katya. "Let's leave it on a few more minutes. Don't you think so, Sveta?"

Sveta agreed.

Finally the girls judged that enough time had passed. The hairdresser unrolled the curlers and thoroughly rinsed Katya's hair. Katya looked in the mirror, then pulled a strand of hair around in front of her face for a closer look.

"Is it going to look better when it's dry?" she asked carefully.

"Oh, yes," the hairdresser assured her. "But remember, you can't wash it for three days."

That night, when Katya went to bed, she dreamed of beautiful hair.

In the morning, she ran eagerly to the mirror. This couldn't be right! Her hair looked like a pile of brown straw, with frizzy, uneven ends. Maybe it just needed to be combed out. But to her shock, when she started to comb, hanks of hair broke off and drifted in clouds to the floor.

"What's the matter with my hair?" she shrieked. As the other girls came running, Katya ran her fingers through her hair. It was brittle.

"Uh-oh!" said Sveta. "We left it too long. Your

hair is burned. Oh, Katya, I'm so sorry."

Katya turned and stared at her friend. Sveta was apologizing. Nobody had ever apologized to Katya in her life. *She* was always at fault. She looked around at the group of girls surrounding her. They all looked sympathetic.

Ana snatched up the scissors. "Here. Sit down, Katya, and I'll trim off the damaged hair. Don't worry; it'll grow out again."

"Yes," said another girl. "In a couple of months, you'll never be able to tell this happened."

"Besides, a shorter style will be cooler," a third girl soothed.

Katya ended up with a very short style indeed. And even then she had to wet it down to keep it from sticking out all around her head like an *oduvanchik* (oh-du-VAN-chik), a dandelion. But when the girls went out to meet the rest of the group, nobody commented on her damaged hair. Even the coach ignored it.

In spite of this disaster, Katya felt good. For the first time in her life she truly felt accepted. She hugged to herself the thought of everyone's kindness and good humor. She was glad she had come to training camp.

After a few more weeks of training, Katya returned to the hairdresser, who made some repairs so Katya did not have to keep wetting her hair down.

Then training was over, and the skiers were given a vacation on the Black Sea. What a wonderful reward for all their hard work! The warm weather reminded Katya of her summers in the Ukraine at Baba Katya's house. Katya loved swimming in the sea and playing games with her friends along the shore.

Too soon the vacation was over, and the campers returned home. When the ski club started up again that winter, Coach Vasilevich had exciting news.

"Children, this year you are going to compete in a cross-country race with several other high schools. Now you must do more than just ski. You must train."

"I thought that's what we were doing," said Katya.

"Oh, no," the coach assured her. "You don't know what training is yet. But you're about to learn."

After that, he worked them harder than ever. They practiced skating on skis to improve their technique. They practiced with double-pole and single-pole stride (and even with no poles) to increase their strength. And they raced and raced with each other.

The weeks passed quickly, and when the day came for the competition, Katya knew that she was at her best. Her group arrived at the race venue in the nearby settlement of Palatka and tumbled out of the bus, looking eagerly around at the flags and the stands and all the people. Many of the children had never before been to such a large settlement or seen so many people in one place.

Katya went to look at the course, which was laid out on top of a hill. She strapped on her skis and began a practice run. The trail was flat, well groomed, and, other than a couple of skate turns, very easy.

At racetime the skiers surged to the starting point. There were so many children that they were all bunched up. Katya found herself in the middle of the pack. She began to work her way toward the outside of the pack of skiers, seeking room to maneuver.

The starting gun fired, and with a loud clashing of skis and poles, the racers set off. Some fell immediately, and Katya had to make a couple of sharp turns to avoid them. She continued to move to the side of the trail. Finally she was able to dig in both poles and push off hard.

Now she was in her element. She kept her hips well forward and her knees loose. She pushed from the shoulder, her stride lengthening as her skis caught the track and she found her rhythm.

Spectators lined the course, shouting encouragement to the skiers and banging metal spoons on pots, but Katya paid no attention to them.

She pushed everything else from her mind and concentrated on maintaining her momentum. She dug in both poles, arms flexed at a constant angle, upper-body weight dropping onto the poles. Stride after stride she increased her speed. Soon there were far fewer people on the track.

When she came to the first skate turn, she lowered her body until she was half sitting. With her arms low and well out front, she pressed down on the tails of her skis, lifted the tip of her left ski, and pushed on her right pole. Swiveling her upper body to the left, she rolled her right ankle inward and pushed hard with her right leg, at the same time swinging her left ski to the left.

As the tip of the left ski touched down on the snow, she brought her right arm and right ski forward. Setting her right ski down next to the left, she double-poled with all her might.

The whole turn was accomplished in much less time than it takes to tell about it, and soon she was racing at full speed again.

The colorful poles marking the kilometers (there are 1.6 kilometers per mile) began to flash past, but Katya refused to pay attention to them. She kept her eyes and mind on the track and on her movements.

The second skate turn was easier because she had more confidence now.

Suddenly the trail was lined with onlookers, and she knew she was near the end. The noise of cheers, applause, and pot-banging was deafening after the long stretch of quiet snow. Katya had to work hard to ignore the crowd and concentrate on her moves.

All at once it was over as she glided across the finish line and pulled herself to a stop. It was only then that she noticed the frantic cheers and arm-waving coming from her school group, and she looked around. Only one other person, a boy, had reached the finish line ahead of her.

Katya's heart beat hard as she watched the other

skiers come in. Several more boys crossed the finish line before any other girl appeared. Although boys and girls ran the race together, they were scored separately. Katya knew that she was the first girl to finish the race. But seconds and then minutes passed, and the winners had still not been announced.

Someone tapped Katya on the shoulder, and she turned to see a race official standing behind her.

"Ekaterina Anatolyevna," he said, using the formal version of her name, "please come with me." Suddenly she felt scared. Such formality could not be good news.

Katya's heart thudded with fright. She must have committed some terrible error. She couldn't think what she had done wrong, but she was obviously about to be disqualified. Maybe even banned from ever competing again. And just when she had discovered that she loved it.

Chapter 6

Skiing Is More Important Than School

Trembling, Katya followed the competition official into a room full of other officials, sitting at a long table. She did not dare look up. She scarcely dared to breathe.

"Ekaterina Anatolyevna, we are faced with a problem," said the man at the head of the table. He voice was grave.

Katya had thought her heart had already sunk as low as it could go, but now she distinctly felt it dropping from her stomach all the way down to her boots.

"You ski so fast that none of the other girls can come close to you. Not only that, but only one boy was able to ski faster than you. Because of this we have decided to evaluate you, not with the girls, but with the boys."

Katya's head jerked up. The official was grinning.

"It is my pleasure to inform you that you have won second place for the district, against all the boy skiers." While Katya was still trying to take it in, another official made the announcement over the public-address system.

The crowd went wild. Katya had never heard such loud cheers. People screamed themselves hoarse while they banged metal spoons on tin pots for several minutes. Nobody could hear anything else, and the officials were forced to wait until the noise died down before they could announce the other medalists.

Back at the bus, Katya's schoolmates mobbed her with hugs, kisses, slaps on the back, and unbridled cheers. Katya knew that she had found her place. She belonged.

A few weeks later, though, she was back in her family's greenhouse, back at her usual chore of carefully pollinating the plants. A greenhouse was necessary on the tundra if one wanted any fresh fruit or vegetables. Plants had to be started early in the greenhouse in order to mature during the short growing season.

When Mama had a day off from her work as an assistant confectioner, she sold the hothouse cucumbers, tomatoes, berries, and other produce at the market.

Not that she was able to keep the money. Papa took everything Mama made and put it under his bunk. He had come to Karamken to make money, and he did everything he could to save so he could return to central Russia and build a big house. Mama still wore the coat she had had when she married him. It was shabby now, worn thin, and not nearly warm enough, but he refused to let her buy a new one.

Now and then Mama managed to hide a little of her money from Papa, but whenever he caught her at it, he beat her. She did not have a good life.

I want a better life, Katya thought as she pushed her hair out of her face. Although it was still freezing outside, the greenhouse, heated by coal fires that were built up every three hours, was a sweltering 40°C (104°F) inside. Katya hated it. So did Hipka. This was one place he refused to follow his mistress.

She blew air up over her face to cool it a bit and moved on to the next plant. With a tiny paintbrush she collected the pollen from the stamen in the middle of a blossom. The pollen gleamed gold, but Katya was not impressed. She painstakingly stroked the brush over the pistils of a blossom on the next plant. She would much rather be outside, skiing around the town with her friends.

At least she would not have to do this much longer. As soon as school was out she would leave for summer ski camp again. Katya was excited at the idea of returning to summer camp. She remembered how happy she had been there last year. She had enjoyed both playing and competing with the other children.

But best of all, whether at summer camp or in competitions, she would be out of reach of Papa's belt.

Katya heard voices just before the door opened. On a breath of fresh air, her parents entered, and with them came Coach Dmitri Vasilevich.

"Coach!" exclaimed Katya, surprised to see him. "Hello."

"Hello, Katya," he said. "I have news for you.

Your performance in cross-country racing has been observed, and your scores have been studied."

Katya wondered what he was leading up to.

"You have been invited to join the Magadan Regional Team," said the coach proudly. "Will you accept and join this team?"

Would she?

"Yes. Of course, I'll be happy to join!" she shouted.

From then on, Katya's life got better. She got to travel, competing against various republics of the U.S.S.R. and meeting new people. At 13 she was the youngest member of the team, and she received special treatment from the coaches. She enjoyed that, too.

But with all her traveling, Katya missed a lot of school, and she was too caught up in training and competition to study much. And then one day her history teacher told the class, "Remember, your paper is due tomorrow."

Her history paper! Katya had forgotten all about it. That night she scribbled out a report. She knew it was bad, but there was no time to research so that she could write anything else. Her face burned with embarrassment when she turned in the paper the next day.

All day long Katya did her best not to think of the horrible paper. She talked and laughed with her friends. Whenever anyone tried to bring up the subject of their history papers, Katya started telling them stories about cross-country ski training and competitions. She had everyone in stitches with her funny stories.

But a couple days later the papers were returned to each student. Katya slid down in her seat and tried not to attract attention as the teacher worked her way closer to her desk. From time to time the teacher urged a student to study harder or to write more carefully. Katya was afraid to hear what her teacher would have to say to *her*.

But when the teacher handed the paper to Katya, she did so with a big smile. Startled, Katya looked down. In big letters across the top of the paper was the word "PASSED." Her jaw dropped, and she darted a look up at her teacher. The teacher smiled again and patted Katya on the shoulder.

"We are so proud of the job you are doing, Katya. You are a credit to Karamken."

Similar incidents occurred with other teachers, and Katya realized that she did not have to worry about studying and working hard in school. Her success on skis would get her through.

But that summer and autumn brought unexpected problems. Because of a knee injury and an eye infection, Katya was not able to train much. As a result, she missed much of the competition season. In March, however, the coach suggested that she participate in the season's last big national cross-country competition, in Magadan. This venue was especially important because four of the skiers would be chosen to participate in the national championship competition in Moscow.

Katya wanted to please her coach, who had done so much for her, so she entered the competition although she did not have much hope for decent results. When she glided onto the course, however, she was surprised at how good she felt and how easy the course was.

The track led through a forest. Katya, used to the treeless tundra, was fascinated by the tall timber. Although, as usual, she did not let herself be distracted by the spectators or other skiers, she could not help looking up at the lofty trees as she slid among them.

She also could not help noticing that she was passing a lot of other skiers. Some of them, she knew, had much higher rankings than she did, but her skis seemed to fly as she poled her way past.

She crossed the finish line to lusty cheers. Coach ran up to her and wrapped her in a big Russian bear hug.

"You have just qualified, my little Katyusha!" he hollered as he beamed at her. "You are going to Moscow!" Katya's head swam with surprise and excitement.

In Moscow Katya outperformed all of her teammates. In fact, she came in third, competing against the best women skiers in all of Russia. Now she had hopes of becoming a real champion.

The next year she increased her competition standing to first place in the Magadan region, her time making her equal with the Russian National Junior Team members. She was jubilant. Though it was a minor achievement compared to the World Championship or the Olympics, she was thrilled. Now she knew what she wanted out of life: gold medals.

The local paper wrote a story about her. When Katya picked up the paper and looked at her own face smiling up at her, she was so proud she wanted to shout. She knew that she had a good future in cross-country skiing. She had no need to waste time worrying about school.

But then she received startling news: she would have to take a geometry test covering three years of work. The standardized test would not be graded by a Karamken teacher, so there was no chance that Katya would get a passing grade because of her skiing. She had to actually pass the test—and she knew nothing about geometry!

In a panic she called on her friend Galya, who was two years older. "Please help me! You're an excellent student. Teach me geometry."

"But the exam is a month from now," protested Galya. "How can you learn three years of geometry in one month?"

"I don't know, but I have to try," Katya wailed.

For the next month the two of them spent every spare moment together. Katya concentrated as never before in her life.

Too soon it was the day of the exam. Nervously Katya entered the room and sat down. The teacher passed out the exam papers. Katya hardly dared to look at her paper, and when she did, she wished she had not. She had received a particularly hard question. Taking a deep breath, she bent her head, picked up her pencil, and began to work.

A few days later the results were posted. Holding her breath, Katya slowly approached the notice board. She quickly found her own name and followed the dotted line across to the score. She checked again, to make sure there was no mistake. Yes, that was her score, all right.

She ran her eyes down the entire list twice. It was true. She had received the highest mark! With a shriek of joy she spun in place. Then she ran off to find Galya and give her the good news.

After that, Katya truly thought school was a waste of time. Why spend three years studying a subject that could be mastered in one month? Once in a while she remembered to study for her induction as a Komsomol member. After all, she did still want to go to the university. But most of the time she was too busy training, competing, or having fun partying with her teammates.

One day, when she was at home for a few weeks, she noticed that Papa was leafing through a book she had never seen before. Other little books were piled on a table near him.

"What are you looking at, Papa?" she asked.

He glanced up. "The Bible."

"How did you get a Bible?" She was surprised. She had never seen a Bible before. Even Baba Katya did not own one.

Papa raised his head and gazed into her eyes.

"Well, it's part of a Bible," he said. "I ordered it from abroad."

Then he told her how he had listened to a Christian radio broadcast in Russian over Voice of America. "One time they offered a free Bible and gave an address. I ordered it, and a month later I received the four Gospels. Just this week a parcel arrived with the Epistles. I also have four little Christian books."

"Have you read them?" asked Katya.

"Oh, no, but I like to look at the pictures."

"Why would you want a Bible?" asked Katya. "What's so important about it?" She certainly had not seen any change in Papa's behavior since he had received the Bible.

"It will help you," said Papa. "For instance, I know you have your high school final exams coming up, and I believe you have not studied very hard for them, have you?"

Katya hung her head.

"Well, you take this." Papa handed her a ribbon. "That's Psalm 91 on one side and an Orthodox saint's prayer on the other. You read these the night before your exam, and I am sure you'll do well."

So that was it. The Bible was a lucky charm. Katya accepted the ribbon, hoping it would help her.

Her first exam was mathematics. The night before the test, Katya picked up the prayer ribbon and began to read: "He that dwelleth in the secret place of the most High shall abide under the shadow of the Almighty . . ."

Chapter 7

The Team Becomes Everything

To Katya's surprise, she did very well on the mathematics exam. Maybe there was something to this Bible and prayer stuff after all!

Then came the chemistry exam. Katya had grown used to taking the easy way, so she glanced at Papa's prayer ribbon, but she did not read it out.

She did all right on her chemistry test, but her results were not at all spectacular.

Katya decided that she had better work harder for her biology exam. She and her friend Lena stayed up all night preparing for the exam. They wrote out answers on little bits of paper for Katya to hide about her person. By the time they were finished, she was far too tired even to think of prayer, let alone read one.

She went into the exam with biology answers tucked in her sleeves, her waistband, and even her socks. But when the exam paper was placed on the desk before her, she was horrified. Not a single question referred to any of the answers she had prepared.

Her exam results were disastrous, and Katya was sure that she had failed because she had not prayed.

She soon had more opportunities to test the power of prayer. She and her father had different views of what was good for a 14-year-old girl. Katya liked to go to the disco and to date boys, but her father was determined to keep her from doing so. He was especially afraid that she would start smoking, and he went at it in his usual violent way.

"If I find you have been smoking, I will cut your lips off!" he warned her. And she believed him.

More than once Papa beat Katya or locked the door and refused to let her in. Sometimes he locked Mama out, too.

"You're too late!" he would call through the door. "No one comes into this house after 9:00 at night!" Then he would stomp off to the bedroom and leave them standing on the doorstep. This could have been deadly in such a cold climate, but they always found a friend who would let them stay for the night.

By now the family had moved to a house slightly larger than the old barracks, and Katya had her own tiny room. If she got home later than her father allowed, she would pause outside the front door.

"Please, God, rescue me from Papa and save me from a beating," she prayed. And it worked! The beatings became fewer and fewer, and finally Papa stopped beating her at all. Katya was sure that this was the result of her prayers.

After her experiences with her exams and her father, Katya thought a lot about the power of prayer.

She eagerly told her friends about her prayers, and they shared her amazement. Not knowing God, they saw prayer as a magic charm.

". . . and then, one evening, when I came home late, instead of beating me, Papa actually gave me a pretty little purse that I had been talking about. He had *never* bought me anything before. He never buys anything for Mama, either." She paused, her eyes bright.

"I tell you, prayer has made this change!"

"Oh, but . . . it's impossible," said Marina. "Isn't it?"

"No, it's not impossible," asserted Katya. "I *know* that God answered my prayers. Maybe it wouldn't hurt to look into religion."

About this same time Katya realized that she was not getting into fights anymore. Maybe she was just too busy with training and competition. Maybe she was too happy with the change in Papa.

Or—could it have something to do with prayer?

But prayer was soon forgotten again as Katya continued to win championships and train for new challenges. The Magadan Regional Championship was coming up again, and several of the girls on the competing Magadan city team were excellent skiers.

Katya's greatest rival was Natasha Bagdanova. The problem was that the regional championship called for skating-style cross-country skiing—Natasha's strong point. Katya was better at classical cross-country style. She had never been able to beat Natasha at skate skiing.

Because of the lineup, Katya started 30 seconds ahead of Natasha. This made it impossible for Katya to tell how well she was doing. So she pushed herself as hard as she possibly could, digging in her poles and throwing her weight from side to side like a speed skater.

To make things harder, the course was lined with spectators making a terrific racket by banging on tin pots. Katya tried hard to ignore the distracting noise and to concentrate on her movements.

Suddenly she saw her coach up ahead. He stepped as close as possible to the ski track and bellowed at her, "You and Natasha! Same time so far!"

There was no time to acknowledge the coach as Katya whipped past the spot where he stood. She just took a deeper breath and pushed harder. As each foot entered a glide, she carefully balanced her weight equally over the whole foot, keeping the same knee bent comfortably as she leaned forward. She was on the last stretch of the course now, a long uphill section.

The cheering and pot-banging got louder, so loud that it hurt Katya's ears. She had to get away from the noise. With one last surge of energy she flew past the roaring crowd.

Once across the finish line, Katya drooped with exhaustion and stood limply, watching the scoreboard. Natasha soon crossed the line, and her time flashed onto the board. Katya whooped and threw her hands into the air. She had beaten Natasha by a full 30 seconds, a huge margin in skiing!

*****

And then Katya's world suddenly and completely changed.

Communism collapsed, and the Soviet Union dissolved into numerous independent republics. Though religion was no longer forbidden, many people feared it because of stories that made Christians out to be monsters.

Katya was not afraid of religion, but like many Russians she was confused, both about the new state of affairs and about religion. She talked about it with her friends Luda, Marina, Galya, and Lena. They were as confused as she.

"I can't believe there is anything good about religion." Luda shook her head. "Our teachers have always told us that all religions are cults. Remember how Galina Stepanovna warned us? And it's true. I just read a book that said Baptists don't baptize children. What they really do is sacrifice them!" Her eyes were wide with horror.

"I don't believe that," said Katya. "I told you before how my prayers helped me. I tell you, praying will protect us. Just think. If we pray, who knows *what* we will accomplish."

They were silent for a moment. Then Galya said, thoughtfully, "Besides, I have heard that the world will end in the year 2000."

"Yes," said Lena excitedly, "and Baba Anna told me that the Bible talks about iron birds at the end of time."

"Those must be airplanes!" exclaimed Marina.

"Baba Yulia told me the Bible talks about 'marked Mikhail,'" said Galya.

"Oh," gasped the other girls.

"Mikhail Gorbachev has a mark on his bald head," said Luda. "Does it mean him? Did you see the part she was talking about?"

"Oh, no," said Galya. "I've never seen a Bible."

"I haven't either," said Luda. "I would be afraid to touch one."

"I've seen one," announced Katya, and they all stared at her. She told them about Papa's Bible. "But . . . I didn't touch it," she admitted.

Luda spoke thoughtfully. "My babushka has told me stories about the bad things that happen to people who don't believe in God."

"So has my Baba Nata," Marina said, surprised.

"My Baba Katya, too," added Katya.

"Of course, it's all just superstition," said Galya, trying to be brave.

"Yes," said Luda, eagerly. "We must not worry about superstition."

"Still," said Marina, thoughtfully, "maybe, just to be on the safe side, we should believe."

"Yes!" agreed the other girls. "Let's believe, just to be safe."

But because they did not really know about God, *believing* did not mean much.

✶✶✶✶✶

Then, when Katya was 17, her life changed again.

When she was competing in Sverdlovsk, Coach Ivan Victorovich Listopad came up to her. "Katya, you must come join the Belarus National Ski Team," he urged.

"Well, I don't know," Katya said slowly. "I've received the same offer from Magadan and Lithuania."

"If you come to Belarus, I can guarantee that you will be accepted into the university," Listopan declared. "I am one of the professors, so I can make it happen. You will not have to worry about taking entrance exams."

Katya nodded. "I'll think about it," she said.

When she returned to Karamken for a visit, the director of the Regional Sports Committee came to persuade her to stay with the Magadan team.

"You must stay in Magadan," he insisted. "We need you. And we will make it worth your while. You will have a free flat of your own. No living in a dormitory." A flat was an apartment. "And you will be automatically accepted into university. No entrance exams for our champion."

Katya talked it over with Lena.

"The university offer is important," said Lena. "Now that there is no more Komsomol, there is no guarantee of getting a university education or a good job."

"I know," said Katya. "In one way, I'm glad, because I don't have to study to become a Komsomol member." Besides, she knew that at this point she would not be able to pass university entrance exams. "On the other hand, everything is so . . . so . . ."

"Uncertain?"

"Yes," Katya admitted. "And things at home are especially bad now. Papa lost everything in the financial chaos after Communism collapsed. He and Mama fight all the time."

Lena gave her a sharp look. "Has he started beating you again?"

"No, but he does hit Mama sometimes. I wish she would leave him." She sighed. "I can't help her, Lena, but I can get out myself."

"So which will you choose?" Lena asked. "After all, they both offer university entrance."

"Well, I'm familiar with Belarus, for my team has trained there a number of times. And I know some of the older Belarus team members who have been recruited from Magadan."

"You don't want to stay in Magadan?" asked Lena, a trifle wistfully, "even if you get a free flat of your own?"

"Definitely not. It's too remote here."

"But Belarus is small—only about 10 million people," Lena protested. "It doesn't have the resources to offer athletes as much as, say, Russia could offer. What about Lithuania? What do they offer?"

"Well, they offer university too. But let's face it. Lithuanians don't like Russians very much. Living there could be very uncomfortable. And while Russia would be good, Moscow has not made me an offer."

"So?"

"So I think it will have to be Belarus."

* * * * *

Soon after Katya left home, her parents separated. Mama went to live with Baba Masha in her village in Tambovr region. Knowing that Mama would never be beaten again, Katya felt free to pursue her own future without worry. The team became her family. They lived together at the university, at training camps, and during competitions. Katya loved every minute of it.

At summer camp, each month she pushed her roller-skis for 1,000 kilometers (more than 600 miles). When the athletes weren't skiing, they were running or pursuing other types of training.

With the team Katya traveled to Finland for training in mountain conditions, covering 800 kilometers (nearly 500 miles) of cross-country snow skiing in a month.

She was in top physical condition, and she felt wonderful. The organization took care of all of her needs. In addition to free room and board and all the clothing and equipment she needed, Katya was given a generous allowance. That left her free to do nothing but concentrate on skiing. Her eyes were on the gold. All she cared about was winning medals.

Although she was enrolled at the university in physical education and in coaching for cross-country skiing, Katya did not have to worry about attending classes. All that counted were the exams. She did take books with her on her training trips, and she studied sometimes, but not seriously. The athletes took their exams separately from the other students, and the exam questions covered their experience as skiers.

And now, no longer restricted by fear of her father, Katya threw herself into the partying life of a pampered athlete. She forgot all about prayer. She loved the parties and the discos—the lights, the people, the dancing. The team took care of all her needs—material and emotional. She did not need God now.

Chapter 8

The Bible Is Real!

One day while looking for something to read, Katya decided to check with Irene (ee-RAY-nah), another skier. Since Irene was a member of a different team, Katya didn't know her well, but she knew that Irene was always reading. Certainly she would have something she could share.

Sure enough, when Katya reached her room she saw that Irene had her head buried in a book. Looking closely, she realized that Irene was reading the Bible, and as she glanced around the room from the security of the doorway, Katya saw other Christian books too.

"What are you doing?" she asked Irene.

The girl looked up. "I'm reading the Bible, as you can see. Why don't you come in, and we can talk about it. I've found that the Bible helps me a lot."

"No, thanks," said Katya. "I don't need the Bible. I was just looking for a book to read."

Irene stood up. "Here, I have several Christian books I can lend you."

By now Katya was hurriedly backing away. "No, no," she said, almost fleeing. And that, she thought, was the end of that. But she was wrong.

After her first year on the Belarus cross-country team, Coach Zamirov moved to Croatia. Coaches changed frequently, and sometimes it was hard to adjust to a new coach, but Katya did her best to get along with each one. She threw herself into her training and was the champion so regularly in Belarus that after a while she did not even bother with tryouts. She did not need to pass the qualifying events.

In the World Championships in Poland she came in eighth, and in Czechoslovakia (now two countries—the Czech Republic and the Slovak Republic), she came in third! She was 19 years old, and she was riding high.

And, of course, after each competition there was a victory celebration, with plenty of vodka.

But suddenly everything began to go wrong. First, Katya overtrained. Her muscles became too tired to repair themselves when at rest, and when she raced they simply let her down.

The first bad result came in the Students' World Championship in Spain. Two years earlier she'd ranked eighth in that competition, and everyone expected her do even better this time. Instead, she came in an embarrassing twenty-second. Katya was devastated.

Then more bad news. Another new coach, Pavel Alexandreyovich, took over the team. Katya did not get along with him at all. For one thing, he was very strict. Then one terrible day, after Katya had partied until very late the night before, the coach called her to his office.

Very carefully, so she wouldn't upset her queasy stomach even more, Katya walked into the room. She had a terrible hangover, and her pounding head was killing her. But her coach looked at her with cold, unsympathetic eyes.

"Katya, I have warned you," he said sternly. "Last night was the second time you have come in drunk. You are off the team. Goodbye."

She couldn't believe it. This couldn't be happening. But the coach stood, ushered her out of the office, and firmly closed the door.

Katya stood in the corridor, stunned. Slowly she pulled herself together and stumbled back to her room—or rather, to what *had been* her room.

Security guards were waiting for her. They stood over her as she packed her belongings and carried them out of the building. The doors shut behind her, and she heard the key turning. She could not take it in. It was not real. She could not be off the team.

But she was. Slowly the realization dawned on her that she had no place to live, no money, and no job. No future! The team had been everything to her, and now it was gone. What would she do?

First, she lurched over to some bushes and threw up.

Then, a sour taste in her mouth, she sat on the building's bottom step with her head in her hands. After a few moments she heard footsteps coming up the sidewalk. The steps hesitated at the end of the walk leading to the building, then changed direction and came her way. They stopped in front of Katya, but she did not look up. She did not want anyone to see her like this.

"Katya?" The voice was hesitant.

Katya grunted in reply.

"Katya, what happened?" Now Katya recognized the voice. It belonged to Irene, the girl who read Christian books. Katya looked up with bloodshot eyes.

"Pavel Alexandreyovich kicked me off the team."

"Oh." Irene did not ask why. Everyone knew that Katya had been warned, and it was obvious that she had been drunk again.

"Where are you going?" asked Irene. Katya looked down at the ground and shrugged. She would *not* cry.

"You can come stay with me," invited Irene.

Katya's head snapped up, though she instantly regretted the movement, as a new wave of nausea seemed to shove her stomach into her throat.

"You'll let me stay with you?" Her voice showed that she hardly believed it. "But—aren't you a Christian?"

"Yes, I'm a Christian," Irene said. "I'm a Seventh-day Adventist."

"But you can't want me to stay with you," Katya muttered. "You know I'm not a Christian, and I'm not interested in being a Christian." She sniffed, wiping her nose with her cuff. "Besides, nobody wants to associate with a troublemaker," she added bitterly.

"Yes, I know all that," Irene said gently, "and I also know that you have no place to go. Jesus said that we should help others. You obviously need help, so you're welcome to stay with me."

The only thing Katya heard in her voice was kindness. At the moment she was too emotionally unstable to express her gratitude, but she pushed herself to her feet and reached for her bags.

"I'll take these," Irene told her. "You concentrate on not being sick."

So Katya moved in with Irene. She learned that Irene was a new Christian. Irene believed in the seventh-day Sabbath, but as a member of a ski team she did not always keep the day holy. Katya also saw her at the team's parties, so she'd never thought too much about Irene's Christianity. But now that they were roommates, Irene began to talk to her about the Bible and Jesus. Katya just shrugged it off, uninterested.

About this time another student in the dormitory read about the importance of a good diet. "You know," she told the other girls, "all the tests and experiments on athletes have shown that athletic performance actually improves on a vegetarian diet."

"Well, I'll never quit eating meat," asserted Katya. "I like it too much."

After two months Irene's coach, a woman, invited Katya to join her team. What a relief! It felt like coming back from the dead. Katya and Irene remained roommates—officially now.

Irene kept inviting Katya to attend church with her, but Katya always refused. She backed away from it as if it would harm her, always telling Irene that she wasn't interested.

Then December arrived, and Katya felt herself covered with a heavy gloom. Christmas was coming, and although she was too old to receive presents from Grandfather Frost, she still longed to spend the time with family. But, she told herself, she no longer had a family. Her parents lived apart, which was best for Mama. And both Mama and Papa lived too far away for her to visit them during the short vacation given the team.

There was nothing that could be done. She would be alone. Right after the big Christmas party at the end of the semester, all the team members would scatter to their own homes.

Katya's Gold

So when Irene invited her home for five days over Christmas, Katya was delighted. She didn't realize that this visit would mark yet another turning point in her life—the most important one of all.

A series of Adventist meetings was being held in Irene's town while the girls were there for the Christmas holiday. Irene invited her roommate to come to the meetings with her, and since Katya felt she owed Irene a debt of gratitude, she agreed to go along and keep her friend company.

To her surprise, the theater in which the meetings were held was so crowded that there was standing room only. In fact, to accommodate all the people who wanted in, each meeting was held twice. Katya, standing in a large crowd in the back at that first meeting, kept jumping up to see over people's heads. She wanted to know what was so interesting that such a large number had come to see.

Evangelist Moses Ostrovsky* talked about things she'd never heard before, concepts such as the Second Coming and what happens after death. It all seemed very strange to Katya, and the terms the evangelist used were foreign to her. But she also found it compelling.

The next evening she and Irene arrived an hour early so that they could find seats.

And when they returned to the university after the holiday and Irene offered Christian books to Katya, she accepted them.

First she read two short books and thought they were good. But when she started reading *Patriarchs and Prophets*, an entire new world opened up for her. Suddenly she realized that this was nothing like her father's religion—a collection of charms and superstitions. And it was much more than a story about saints whose lives were so far from reality that nobody could relate to them.

Galina Stepanovna and her other teachers had insisted that the Bible was just a collection of myths. But this was history! This was *real*.

As Katya continued to read the Adventist books, she became convinced that some meats were unclean, and she cut them out of her diet. Also, she began to see how God has acted throughout history.

Katya began to change. Alcohol lost its appeal for her, and she decided she wouldn't drink anymore.

Katya and Irene had been training apart from the other skiers, so it was some time before the others discovered Katya's determination not to drink. By the next year she'd returned to the Belarus team, and when they began collecting money to buy vodka and other liquor for the usual big Christmas party, Katya did not contribute to the fund.

"Hey, Katya," one of her teammates complained, "what's the matter with you? Everyone else is chipping in for the party, but you aren't. Why not?"

"I won't drink," Katya told her, "so there's no point in my paying for alcohol."

"*You* won't drink!" they hooted. "That'll be the day!"

At the party her teammates watched her closely. When they saw that she really did not drink anymore, they were finally convinced that she meant what she said.

The competition season ended in April, and Katya began looking for an Adventist church in nearby Minsk.

Eventually she was told of one, but the dark-green building she found did not look promising. The ground floor housed a community center, where people came for chess and social activities. The place reeked of tobacco smoke.

The church was, indeed, located in this building, but it was upstairs. The inside of the building was so dark that Katya found it hard to stay awake. This was about as different as she could imagine from a bright, ornate Orthodox church with its golden crosses and jeweled icons.

Katya sat with some other young women who complained that the pastor was a poor speaker and that the light was not good. Both were true, but Katya didn't care. She had come to learn about God, and it seemed as though God closed her senses to the unpleasant surroundings so that she was not distracted from what she heard.

The friends she made at church were vegetarians, and that reminded her of the studies on performance. Of course, she wanted to do her best in competition. Gradually she cut out red meat, then chicken, and finally fish. To her surprise, she was happy as a vegetarian.

She began to promote vegetarianism among her teammates. Naturally they wanted to turn in their best performances too. Soon several of them became vegetarians.

When they traveled, it became Katya's job to order their food. They ate a lot of nuts, peas, beans, and caviar. Katya was careful to keep their diet balanced and full of tasty food.

One time the team spent four months in Italy, and Katya ordered beans so frequently that hotel and restaurant cooks started to call her "Mrs. Bean."

Often when she went to a restaurant, the serving staff would not bother waiting for her to order. "You want some pease porridge [pea soup]," they would say.

Sometimes the hosts of various competitions would offer the athletes meat, but Katya would always say a polite "No, thanks."

She was almost surprised at how well and happy she felt, but the coaches were not so sure.

"Are you sure this is a good idea?" they asked. "Don't you need meat to give you strength? We don't want you to falter at a critical time."

But soon they were singing a different tune.

"The entire team is performing better than ever before," said one coach after another. "You go right ahead and be vegetarians."

---

*Currently president of the Belarus SDA Conference.

Chapter 9

Soon Katya invited a couple of university friends to attend church with her. Right after they both accepted her invitation, Katya had to leave for a competition. While she was gone, her friend Natasha found the church on her own and began attending and, when Katya returned, all three went to church together. After a while the one friend told them, "This is not for me," and she stopped going. But Natasha continued to go every Sabbath.

Then someone invited Natasha and Katya to join a Bible study group that met each week an hour before church. They had to travel for one and a half hours to get to the church by 9:00 a.m. for the Bible study, but they were so eager to learn that they didn't care about the inconvenience.

As she learned more about Jesus, His sacrifice and His forgiveness, Katya felt her heart change. She found, for instance, that she no longer hated Papa. She could forgive him as Christ had forgiven her.

A few weeks after Katya and Natasha joined the study group its members started talking about the baptism that was coming up in a couple weeks. They were going to be baptized. Katya hadn't realized that this was a baptismal study group, but she decided she wanted to be baptized too.

She wrote to her parents to tell them of her decision, and they were shocked. Papa was too far away to stop her, so he sent a frantic telegram: "Don't go there!"

The telegram did not change Katya's mind. She talked to Natasha. "Have you decided to be baptized?"

"I would like to, but I'm not sure . . ." Natasha wavered.

"Listen, Natasha, when you make a decision for Christ, the devil doesn't have power over you. If you hold back, the devil can still claim you. Is that what you want?"

"No, of course not," Natasha protested. And before long she told Katya that she'd decided to be baptized with her and the others.

The baptism took place on a lovely day in May. Lacking a proper baptismal tank, the church used a sauna for the service. The sauna was small and dark, but Katya and Natasha were happy to know that they had joined God's family.

They were so happy that it was a shock when they returned home to find that a sudden hailstorm had broken a mirror in Natasha's room.

"What does this mean, Katya?" asked Natasha. "The weather was fine when we left. What caused this sudden storm?"

"I don't know," answered Katya. "Perhaps the devil is angry because we were baptized." But they decided that if the devil *had* caused the storm, they were not going to let him frighten them away from God.

Eager to share her newfound faith, Katya went to visit Mama and Baba Masha in their Tambov village. She began to tell them about her beliefs.

Baba Masha was horrified. "No, no, Katya! Don't have anything to do with them. They are a cult. I *know* it. You will become a human sacrifice. Have I told you about the time I was nearly killed as a sacrifice?"

"Yes, Baba Masha," Katya said gently, "but Adventists are not cultists. They do not sacrifice people. Their religion is real. It is not just rituals."

Baba Masha, who followed many Orthodox religious rituals, was not convinced.

Neither was Mama. "Their beliefs are so strange," she argued. "Take this business of worshipping on Saturday. Everyone knows that Sunday is the day to go to church."

"Sunday is not the day the Bible calls the Sabbath," countered Katya.

Mama and Baba Masha continued to argue with her over doctrine, but they could not change her mind. When it was time for Katya to leave, she left a Bible and the Conflict of the Ages Series with them.

"A Bible," marveled Baba Masha. "I have never read a Bible."

Next, Katya traveled to the Ukraine. At first, Baba Katya was delighted that her namesake had become a Christian.

"Frozina and Annychka have become Christians too," bubbled the old woman when Katya visited her. She also told Katya of several other villagers who had taken their stand for Christ. But she sobered when Katya said that she was a Seventh-day Adventist.

"Oh, Katya, couldn't you have joined the Orthodox Church? Why did you have to become a Stunde?"

Stunde is the German word for "hour." It came from the old days and referred to the time Russian Protestants of German extraction set aside for Bible study. In Baba Katya's village the term had eventually come to be applied to Seventh-day Adventists.

Katya was not going to argue with her grandmother about what church she should attend. "Baba Katya, I brought you a present," she said, pulling a Bible out of her bag. "It's in Ukrainian," she added.

Baba Katya's wrinkled face broke into a huge smile as she accepted the Bible, lovingly stroking the cover of the holy book with trembling fingers. Her eyes grew moist.

"This is the first time I have seen a Bible since Stalin confiscated them all," she murmured reverently. "Thank you, Katya. This is the most wonderful present I have ever received. I will put it in a place of honor."

*****

With her baptism Katya felt that she now belonged to two teams, God's team and the cross-country ski team. She was glad that her ski team's first 21-day training cycle would begin on Sunday. That meant they would get Sabbath off each week, and during the last week of the month the athletes always got a rest break. But the next month, the cycle would begin on a different day. This meant that the following Saturday would be a training day.

Determined to keep the Sabbath, Katya talked to her coach.

"I cannot train on Saturdays," she explained. "I am a Seventh-day Adventist Christian now. I believe in the Bible Sabbath, and I must keep it."

To her surprise, the coach readily agreed to let her have Sabbaths off during the training season. One of the other coaches joked, "I've decided to become a Muslim and take Fridays off. I like this religion stuff. You get to do whatever you want."

But it was not quite as easy as that.

To begin with, Katya had to travel for up to three hours to get to church and then another three hours back to the training camp after the services. She began to lose sleep. In addition, she had to make up her training while the other athletes had their weekly day off. But she was determined to honor God.

The coaches thought that this was just a phase. "You go from one extreme to another, Katya," said one. "You'll get over this, too."

But when Katya remained steadfast, the head coach lost patience. "Choose the team or the church," he snapped at her. "Talk to your church members and make an agreement with them that you will train on Saturday sometimes."

Of course, Katya knew it did not work that way. She prayed with her church friends and then went to the Olympic Committee.

"You told me to make a choice. I see it as a choice between the team and God. I choose God."

Suddenly the committee members realized that she was serious. "Oh, now," they said, "you've just signed a two-year contract. You can't quit. We'll give you your Sabbaths. Our first training camp starts on Saturday. You have to be present, but you don't need to work out."

But how could she even go to the training camp on Sabbath? Katya lost more sleep as she thought about the decision she must make. Could she serve God if she went to the camp? Maybe she could influence her teammates if she just sat and read the Bible while they trained.

Oh, what should she do?

The departure point for the drive to the training camp was near the church. Katya met with church members and prayed. After praying, she knew what she must do. She left her belongings on the bus and went to church instead of to the training camp. It was still summer, and the days were long, so the church had both morning and evening services.

After the evening service Katya returned to the dorm and found Irene there. Irene had gone to the training camp because she was afraid of being cut from the team.

"Coach was very angry that you didn't show up," Irene told Katya. "He was shouting, 'We just have to kick her out! It's so annoying when everybody else is here and she's not!'"

Katya prayed some more. The next morning she prayed silently as she rode the bus with her teammates to the training camp.

"Katya, where have you been?" the coach asked cheerfully.

"I was in church, of course," she answered.

"You know you were supposed to be here," he said, but there was no anger in his voice.

"Yes," said Katya, "but I was in church."

The other athletes stared, openmouthed, at the coach's calm demeanor after his temper tantrum of the day before. They all went back to training, with nothing more said.

Competition season, however, presented a new problem for Katya. Virtually all of the competitions were scheduled on Saturday or Sunday. She believed in the Sabbath, but could she keep it while competing? On the other hand, how could she let the team down? She wavered.

"I'm part of the team. I can't say, 'I'm not competing today,'" Katya rationalized. "Besides, I'm witnessing for Christ to my teammates all the time. If I were kicked off the team, I couldn't witness anymore."

Katya tried to compromise, to be loyal to both God and the ski team. She loved both. The team was her home and her family. God was her newly discovered, loving Father. So although she felt uncomfortable about it, she did sometimes compete on Sabbath.

As she traveled with the team, though, she tried to make each Saturday seem as much like Sabbath as possible. She would tell her teammates, "Today is Sabbath, so we will listen only to Christian music." And they did what she said.

In the meantime, she did all she could to tell others about Christ. At hotels she talked to the housekeepers, administrators, and receptionists. She told them how much joy she felt since knowing Christ.

She took Christian books and videos with her and handed them out. Often, when she returned to her room, she would find a housekeeper listening to a video while cleaning the room.

She gave her teammates books and videotapes of sermons, music, and seminars. Not everyone read the books, but some did. Sometimes even members of the men's team read what she brought.

One time a coach came to her. "Do you have anything to read?" he asked. "I don't have anything."

She gave him a copy of the pamphlet *Truth or*

Propaganda, and he read it twice.

When the team went to Italy for the World Cup, Katya had a special opportunity to introduce her teammates to Jesus.

The athletes flew to the competition, and the coaches drove a minivan with all the skis and equipment.

The athletes settled into their hotels and waited. And waited. They waited all day, and the coaches did not arrive. They waited another day. Still no coaches. The team had no skis, no training sessions. The hotel personnel wondered what was going on. The team members had to stand idly by and watch their rivals preparing for the competition.

Finally Katya suggested they pray. Following her lead, the team members stood in a circle and prayed that their coaches would soon arrive.

Two hours later someone shouted, "They're here! The coaches have arrived!"

The team members flew out of their rooms and ran out to where the coaches were climbing out of the minivan.

"What happened? Where have you been? We prayed for you to get here," called the athletes.

"The minivan broke down. We had to wait for repairs," explained the coaches. Everyone was relieved that the incident had turned out well. They hoped the delay would not hurt their performance in the competition.

Chapter 10

Everything for Jesus

The team's performance in the World Cup was everything they could have hoped for. Their top scorer was Elena Sinkevich. She was a favorite of everyone, and Katya was happy for her. Katya was also happy to be ranked second only to Elena.

Both were overjoyed when the coach informed them, "You two will go to the Olympics in Nagano, Japan."

And just before the team left for Nagano, Belarus president Alexander Lukashenko honored them at a banquet. Katya's Adventist friend Oksana had a suggestion. "Katya, why don't you take the Conflict of the Ages Series to the banquet as a gift for the president?"

"Oh, that would be a waste of time. There's no way they would let me present the books," argued Katya.

"You never know what might happen," Oksana said.

So Katya put the books in her bag, and as the banquet drew to a close, she sought out the president's assistant.

"I have a gift I would like to give President

Lukashenko in appreciation for his support of the team. Would that be all right?"

"Yes, sure," replied the assistant. "What is the gift?"

"Some religious books."

"That's fine. Did you sign them?"

"Oh, no. I didn't think of that."

"Why don't you sign them right now? Here, you may use my pen."

Katya took the pen and signed each book, wishing the president a great term of office and the wisdom of Solomon.

"Very good," said the assistant. "I will give these to the president. It is very thoughtful of you. The president will certainly appreciate it."

And then, almost before she knew it, Katya was on her way to the Olympics. The Olympics! She was so excited, it hardly seemed necessary to take a plane. She was almost happy enough to fly to Japan on her own.

She looked around the airplane's cabin. Everyone else was excited too. The free liquor was flowing liberally, but they all knew better than to urge any on her. As an Adventist Christian, she would never drink again, and they knew it.

Victor, the head coach, had the seat next to hers. The more he drank, the looser his tongue became. Suddenly he turned to her.

"Katya, you said you're an Adventist, but you're really not."

Startled, Katya stared at him. "Why . . . ? " was all she could get out.

"Because you don't keep Sabbath."

The words were a knife in her heart.

Katya knew that the coach was right. She had not been keeping the Sabbath faithfully. She had been trying to have it both ways, but it was impossible to serve both God and the world.

"I'll quit after the Olympics," she said, the words choking her.

The coach was not ready to give in. "Oh, of *course,*" he sneered. "*After* the Olympics. You wouldn't quit *before.*"

Katya sat stunned and miserable. The trip was ruined. No matter how she did in competition now, she would be unable to take any pleasure in it.

The second day in Japan, Coach Victor came up to Katya, accompanied by a huge man in his 50s. The coach had forgotten his scathing words on the flight over.

"Katya," he greeted her cheerfully, "I have met a sports pastor. This is Carl Dambman; he's a former heavyweight wrestler.

"He's an American, but he's been living in Russia. In fact, he's the director of the Sports Ministry in Moscow. Carl, this is Katya Antaniuk, one of our star cross-country skiers."

"Katya," said Carl. "I understand that you're a Christian."

"Yes, I am."

"Good. There's an interfaith religious center here in Olympic Village. We can discuss the Bible, watch Christian movies, and pray. All the Christian athletes are invited. In fact," he glanced at Victor, "anyone who wants to come is welcome."

"I have a meeting," said Coach Victor, backing away. "You two enjoy getting acquainted." He hurried off down the hall.

"Would you like to come to the center, Katya?" asked Carl.

"Sure," she agreed. "Irene will want to go too. And there may be others."

Others did want to go. In fact, all the Russian women athletes went to the religious center that Sunday, even those from other sports.

"You know," Carl said to Katya and Irene after the meeting, "I would like to go to church here in Nagano and give my testimony. Christianity isn't growing much in Japan, and I think it would do the church members good to hear from other Christians. Would you like to go too?"

The two young women enthusiastically agreed, and Carl called the Baptist church to ask for a car to pick them up the next Sunday.

As the car started off Sunday morning with a full load of young people, Katya could not help asking the driver, "Is there a Seventh-day Adventist church in Nagano?"

"I really don't know," said the driver.

A young Japanese man sitting in the back spoke up. "I'm an Adventist."

Katya stared. An Adventist in a Baptist church car? What was he—an angel?

When they reached the Baptist church, the Japanese SDA called the Adventist church and made arrangements for Katya to attend prayer meeting later in the week.

On the appointed evening Carl and a couple of others went with Katya and Irene to the SDA church. Carl interpreted for the two Russians.

After the meeting Pastor Masuo Ikemasu came up to Katya and Irene. "Would you be willing to give your testimony in church this Sabbath?" he asked.

"Yes, certainly. We would be delighted," they responded.

But Irene was thoughtful on the way back to the Olympic Village, where they were roommates. When they were back in their room, she finally spoke.

"Katya, how are we going to give our testimony? We can't speak Japanese, and Carl said he can't come with us to translate this time."

"Yes, it is a problem," admitted Katya. They thought, talked and prayed about the problem for the next couple of days. Sabbath was coming up shortly. What could they do?

"I know!" Katya had a sudden inspiration. "I'll go ask the Belarus Olympic officials for an interpreter."

Happily, she sped off to the office and made her request. To her delight, the officials found Tomoko,* a Japanese woman who spoke Russian and was willing to go to church with them.

On Sabbath Pastor Ikemasu picked up the three young women for church. Katya was glad that there was no Sabbath conflict at these games.

As Katya and Irene gave their testimony, Tomoko occasionally looked puzzled. She did not understand a lot of the terms, such as "the Second Coming."

When she got to such a place, she would translate the term into Japanese, then look to the pastor. Pastor Ikemasu would explain the term and its place in Adventist belief.

At the end of the service Tomoko said, "I would like to attend an Adventist church when I go back home after the games. Do you know where I could find it?" Pastor Ikemasu gladly looked up the address for the church in her city.

All of this only strengthened Katya's determination to follow Christ completely.

Her competition score at Nagano was in the middle, which was quite respectable for a first-time Olympian. But competing for medals had lost its allure. Earthly gold could not begin to compete with the heavenly gold she now lived for.

After the Olympics there was one more competition, this one in Russia.

"I'm not going to take you to this one," Coach

Victor said bluntly. "You're just going to resign at the end of your contract anyway."

But Victor Shepelevich, the Olympic Committee member who had hired Katya, had other ideas. He called Katya to his office. "Why doesn't your head coach want to take you to the competition?" he asked.

"Because I'm quitting the team."

"Quitting the team!" He was shocked. "Why are you quitting the team?"

Tearfully Katya explained that she had to make a choice. As much as she enjoyed skiing, and as much as she loved her team members, she felt that staying with them would be turning her back on God. She must choose God.

Shepelevich was an atheist, but he was touched by her loyalty to God.

"Very interesting," he said. "I want to hear more about this."

After their meeting, Shepelevich called Katya's coach. "You have to take Katya Antaniuk to the competition," he ordered, "or you will have problems."

Katya's last competition was her best. She won a gold medal and a title: Master of Sport at an International Level. The only higher title was that given to the top contenders in the World Cup, World Championship, or Olympic Games.

But titles and gold medals no longer held first place in her life or in her heart. She prepared herself to notify the Minsk Region Olympic Committee that she was quitting. It was much harder than she had imagined. The committee members were shocked and dismayed. They tried to talk her out of it.

"Can't you get a dispensation to let you compete on Sabbath?" they asked.

"I'm sorry," Katya replied. "It doesn't work that way. I must do what the Bible says."

"But you can't quit!" exclaimed one.

"We will make it worth your while to stay," said another.

"Yes, we will give you your own free flat," promised a third.

"I'm sorry," Katya repeated. "You have all been good to me, and I have enjoyed being part of the team. But I see it as a choice. I must choose God."

Finally, they reluctantly accepted her resignation. She was in tears as she walked out of the room. This was the hardest thing she had ever done.

But it was the right thing. She dashed away her tears, stood up straight, and marched down the street. She would not grieve. She had chosen Christ, and that was the best thing anyone could do.

From now on, God was her family, her home, and her support. She would trust in Him.

---

*Actual name unknown.

Chapter 11

More Choices

After leaving the team, Katya visited her mother and Baba Masha in Tambov. The first thing she noticed when she walked into their house was that the religious icons had been removed from all but one of the corners.

"Baba Masha," asked Katya, "why did you remove your icons?"

"I didn't know before, but I read the Bible you gave me. Now I know it's wrong to worship images."

"Then why is one still here?" Katya was puzzled.

"Exactly what I told her," said Mama. "Here, Katya, you take it."

"No," protested Baba Masha. "I can't throw that one out. It was a gift from my mother."

"If it is wrong to have them, it is wrong to have even one," Katya argued. Baba Masha looked from her granddaughter to the icon, then back to Katya.

"All right," she said at last. "Throw it out."

"No," Katya said. "*You* throw it out."

Baba Masha looked into Katya's eyes for a long time. Then she took a deep breath, grabbed the icon, and tossed it into the trash.

This time while Katya was visiting, Baba Masha suffered heart seizures. At the same time, a Pentecostal Christian visited the village. He came to people's homes, playing his guitar and preaching.

"Do you want to be healed?" he asked Baba Masha. "I can heal you with prayer."

Of course she wanted to be healed. "I believe with all my heart that God can heal me," Baba Masha told him.

The next time he visited, the preacher prayed for her, and she was healed. As a result of this experience, Baba Masha and Mama decided to be baptized into the Pentecostal church.

Katya wasn't so sure. *Is this the right thing for them to do?* she wondered. She prayed about it and began to study Pentecostal books. As she studied, she realized that the books contained many biblical errors. How could she convince Mama and Baba Masha of these errors? She didn't know.

"Katya," said Mama, coming in the door one afternoon, "the Pentecostal pastors want us to bring you to the church next time we go."

"Oh, Mama, I don't want to get into an argument with them," said Katya.

"Ha!" teased Baba Masha, her eyes twinkling. "Are you afraid to hear what they have to say? You are always ready to talk about what you believe. Why don't you listen to someone else?"

"I'll pray about it," Katya promised.

"Good," said Mama. "Come, and we'll have supper now."

Katya shook her head. "No, thanks," she murmured. "I think I'll fast."

And so she fasted and prayed, "Dear Lord, please give me the right answers to their arguments. Call to my mind the truths I have studied in the Bible." And as the days passed, she reviewed the biblical passages that had become precious to her.

Katya went with her mother and grandmother to the next meeting at the church. Several pastors were there, ready to confront her. As she had feared, the "discussion" quickly degenerated into a debate. The pastors became more strident as Katya used the Bible to counter all their arguments.

The pastors were especially upset when they saw some of their church members nodding their heads in agreement with Katya's statements. The whole thing ended with Katya standing in the middle of the group of pastors, waving her arms in wide gestures as she gave her testimony, while the silent church members looked on.

"That did it," Baba Masha told Katya as they walked home. "You were so certain of your Bible proofs, and the pastors had such weak arguments. I am not going to be baptized into that church."

Katya breathed a silent prayer of thanks to God.

A couple of days later a whole family from the

Pentecostal church arrived at the house. "Please teach us all about your beliefs," they begged Katya. So she spent the entire day preaching to them and answering their questions.

To Katya's great joy, both Mama and Baba Masha soon decided to be baptized into the Adventist Church. The nearest one was 100 kilometers (62 miles) away. Katya called the pastor to tell him the good news. And so he gathered several people from other villages who were awaiting baptism, and baptized the whole group in the river.

Back at the house there was something else that troubled Katya. It was the question of Baba Masha's vodka. Baba Masha did not drink the liquor, but she kept two cases of it on hand to pay the handyman. Nobody in the village would do anything without pay, and with cash scarce, vodka had become the main form of barter.

"You must get rid of the vodka," Katya said.

"What will we do?" asked Mama, dismayed. "How will we get along?"

"We cannot do that work ourselves," protested Baba Masha.

"We will trust in God," said Katya. "If it is wrong to drink liquor, then it is wrong to give it to others." She grabbed a bottle of vodka and began pouring its clear contents into the toilet.

"No!" cried Baba Masha. "We must have the vodka. It is currency." She rushed forward to take the bottle from Katya, but Mama held her back.

"Katya is right," said Mama quietly. "We must have faith." Katya continued to open bottles and pour out the liquor until all of the vodka was gone.

And God rewarded their faith, just as He has promised, and as He always does. A neighbor began to help them without asking for any pay. And on Friday nights he filled in for Mama at her job at the recreational center. In her place, he opened the doors, got out the recreational equipment, set up projectors, and did whatever else was needed.

In return Mama sometimes cooked for him, and she cared for him when he was ill and those times when he fell into a drunken stupor. They continued this arrangement until Mama retired from the job five years later and the neighbor died.

In the meantime, Katya left to attend school. She had no money, but with the help of Adventists in Russia, Japan, and the United States she was able to attend the Zaoksky Theological Seminary, located about 100 kilometers (62 miles) from Moscow. Now, however, her former carelessness about school caught up with her, and she had a lot of studying to make up. This time she put her whole being into studying and learning the things she had missed along the way. It was hard, but with God's help, she caught up.

A few months later Papa came to see her, very worried that his daughter had gotten involved in what he thought was a religious cult. When he arrived, he was very suspicious and cautious. He questioned everything he saw and heard.

Then Katya introduced him to Gena, a friend from Belarus. Gena, who was a theology student, had an extra bed in his room, so he invited Papa to stay with him. The two men spent a lot of time talking, and after a few days Papa began to relax.

When it was time for him to leave, he told Katya that being at the college had been an amazing experience. "I see so many young people here who really believe," he said. "Their faith is real. Some of them were drug addicts and alcoholics before, but they have changed. Now I know that this faith of yours is real."

Katya's heart overflowed with thankfulness when he added, "Will you pray for me before I leave?"

Joyfully Katya knelt and prayed earnestly for Papa. When she opened her eyes, she was shocked to see tears running down his face. She had never in her life seen him cry.

A couple of months later Papa wrote to Katya and said that he hoped God would change his life too. He has not yet accepted Christ as his Savior, but Katya continues to pray for him.

While at the seminary Katya contacted Boris Gertsen, a filmmaker who produced Olympic documentaries. She asked him for copies of videos of her competitions he had made.

"Sure," said Boris, "I'll be glad to get them to you. What are you doing now, anyway?"

When Katya told him how she had found God, he wanted to make a documentary of her story. She agreed, thinking that this was a way to reach people who might never otherwise hear about God. So she went to the studio, as he had asked her to do. In the meantime he had had a new idea.

"Let's make a live program at your church."

This was a remarkable request. Other than the Orthodox Church, religious organizations were not allowed to do such things. But Gertsen did not seem worried.

So the next time Katya went to church, Gertsen sent along a film crew and director. They stood outside the building as the narrator asked her questions about her religious experience. Then the camera filmed her walking up the steps and into the church.

Before the crew left, Katya gave Christian books to each one of them. Unfortunately, she didn't have an opportunity to see the film, because it came out while she was traveling. She just hoped that someone who saw it would be stirred to learn about God.

That winter Katya and Carl Dambman went as chaplains to the World Championship in Ramsau, Austria. Katya roomed with her old friend, Elena Sinkevich, while she was there. Elena did very well at the World Championship Games, coming in sixth. When she returned to Minsk, President Lukashenko personally congratulated her. Katya was very happy for her friend.

But a month later Katya was shocked to learn that Elena had committed suicide, hanging herself with her husband's belt. As soon as she could, Katya talked with other women from Elena's team.

"For the past few months," said one, "Elena seemed depressed. Several times I heard her say: 'I have everything. I have reached success. I have a flat, a car, money, a family. But it doesn't bring me joy. I feel sometimes that I don't want to live anymore.'"

Katya grieved for her friend. And she prayed, "Thank You, God, for giving me something to live for."

Katya had given up her team family, trusting that God's people would be a family for her, and her faith was rewarded. Church members from Russia, Japan, the United States, Scotland, Switzerland, and England rallied to Katya's aid at various times, making her feel loved and accepted. But God had even better plans for her.

Papa had remarried, and his new wife had a teenage daughter named Marina. Katya and Marina became close friends and real sisters.

Eventually Marina, too, was baptized into the Adventist Church and attended Zaoksky Seminary. She later spent a semester as a missionary in Thailand.

Katya's hard work at the seminary paid off. She graduated magna cum laude, "with high honors," earning both a secretarial diploma and a theology degree.

She learned that Mama and Baba Masha had begun holding meetings in their home with interested villagers. The two women always gave out whatever reading material they had. In fact, there was such a demand for literature that Mama began buying multiple subscriptions to Adventist magazines so that she could share them with the other villagers. She also gave several videos and books to the director of the local collective farm.

Not everyone was happy with these efforts, however. Some of the villagers resisted any new ideas. They still feared cults. A few even went further than angry looks and words. One man threatened to burn their house down. Of course, the women prayed for protection, and before the angry man could carry out his plans, he died of a heart attack.

When one of the village women decided that she wanted to be baptized, her husband objected strenuously. He often came to the house when the women were studying the Bible. Drunkenly he would wave huge knives in their faces and threaten, "I'll kill all of you!"

The frightened women would pray, "Dear God, please protect us from this drunken man." He would stand there, staring at them with wild, bloodshot eyes, then suddenly turn and stumble out. He never harmed them, and his wife was baptized.

* * * * *

Eventually Katya was able to attend Newbold College in England, studying for a master's degree in theology while acting as sports coordinator for the college.

In 2006 she went to Turin, Italy, for the Winter Olympics, not as a competitor, but as the first Seventh-day Adventist chaplain. She made numerous contacts with the athletes, praying with them, renewing old friendships, and distributing New Testaments and other literature. She even found herself witnessing to her fellow chaplains.

When they asked her why she had quit her team, she explained her conviction that she must keep the Sabbath. A couple of the chaplains asked her other doctrinal questions, and she answered as carefully and thoughtfully as she could.

One in particular came to her for answers to the theological questions that bothered him. *As if I were an expert,* thought Katya, and prayed for God to give her wisdom. She was always happy to discuss her views with him and to point him to the Bible for answers to his questions.

"You know," he finally said, "I like the idea of the Sabbath. From now on I'm going to keep it too. Thank you, Katya."

Grateful for her efforts at Turin, the chaplains also invited her to join them at the 2008 Summer Olympics in Beijing and the 2010 Winter Olympics in Vancouver.

Meanwhile Katya returned to Newbold to continue her work and studies there.

Chapter 12

When God Leads

One chilly November day, as Katya took her place in the cafeteria at Newbold College, she noticed a new face, a young man. At one point their eyes met, and he twinkled at her. A few days later she found herself at the same table with him.

"Hi, I'm Katya," she said.

"Paolo Marzano," he responded with an eager smile. At first, his English was not good enough to enable them to converse, but every time he saw Katya, he smiled. Whenever she went to the cafeteria, she saw him looking at her, and she looked back. He seemed to be as smart as he was handsome. And he was watching her eagerly.

The next Sabbath she found herself sitting next to him in church. He kept turning to smile at her, which made her heart beat faster.

As Paolo's English improved, they began to talk more and more. Katya discovered that he was working on his Ph.D. in geotechnical engineering, and he had come to Newbold to study English for several weeks.

After that, they often sat at the same table and enjoyed long talks.

One day Paolo was especially excited. "Someone told me you skied in the Olympics," he said.

"Yes, I did," said Katya.

"I am in a hurry to get to class right now, but please tell me all about it soon."

So one evening she told him about her experience in Japan.

Paolo listened intently and asked questions that showed he understood the sport. "I'm a great sports fan," he told her when she had finished her story. "In fact, I used to participate in a lot of sports activities myself. My specialty was the high jump. The height of my success came when I was 16. I was five feet six inches tall, and I jumped six feet high."

"You don't compete anymore?" Katya asked him.

"No," he said, regretfully. "Once when I was competing at hurdling, I hit a bar and injured my knee. My kneecap wound up in the middle of my thigh!" Katya knew the injury must have been terribly painful, but Paolo just laughed. "It's over," he said. While he'd had surgery to repair the knee, he'd never been able to compete professionally again.

"But I love sports, and I'm impressed with your accomplishments," he said, turning the conversation back to her.

Katya was impressed that Paolo was as modest as he was smart and handsome. She learned that he taught at a university and had been involved in some major engineering projects, including two subway lines in Rome, a big harbor, and a railway.

Paolo gazed deeply into her eyes. "I am amazed," he said, "amazed at your beauty and at your sports ability. You are such an interesting person!"

At this, Katya found she was having trouble breathing. *But I don't really know him*, she reminded herself. *We've just met.*

After that, though, Paolo always saved a place for her at the cafeteria table where he sat. As they talked, they kept finding more things they had in common. In no time they had become firm friends. They spent a lot of time talking, and everywhere Katya went she found Paolo near her.

She began to show him around the area surrounding Newbold. Just before he had to return to Italy, Katya drove with him to the romantic town of Henley on Thames. There they walked and talked for hours.

After Paolo returned to Italy, they often talked on the phone. One time they talked for nine hours straight!

In February he returned to England for a few days. He'd come to see friends, he said, but he spent most of his time with Katya. "I miss you," he told her. "I cannot stay away from you." He decided to take part of his Ph.D. at nearby Cambridge University so that they could see each other often. In April they officially began dating, and their relationship developed quickly.

Then, one day in August, he took her back to Henley on Thames, where they had spent those enjoyable hours several months before. They strolled onto the romantic bridge that spanned the river.

"I think of this as our place," he told her. "I've thought of it often since that time you brought me here."

Suddenly he dropped to one knee. "Katya, will you be my wife?" he asked earnestly.

She smiled with her whole heart. "Yes, Paolo, I will."

From his pocket he took out a small pink padlock on a chain. The lock had both their initials on it.

"Our relationship is the padlock," he said as he handed her a key. "We both have a key to open the lock and leave if we want.

"The chain symbolizes God, who is on the throne of our relationship," he continued as he wrapped the chain around the railing and fastened it with the padlock.

Then he flung his key as far as he could, out across the river. It plopped into the water, many yards away.

"I don't need a key because I never want to unlock the padlock. I promise my entire life to you. I will always be with you," he promised.

"I don't need a key either," said Katya. "I promise my life to you," and she tossed her key after his.

That same month they visited her family in

Russia, and then his family in Italy. All the parents were delighted with their future in-laws. At first the couple planned to marry soon after Katya completed her master's degree. But one day as they considered a wedding date, Katya's brow furrowed.

"What is the matter?" asked Paolo, ever alert to her expression.

"It's just that last year I had such trouble with my visa. It expired, and I had to return to Russia. For a while there I thought I wouldn't get a new one and wouldn't be able to return to Newbold. What if that happens again—before we are able to marry?"

"I know the solution to that!" exclaimed Paolo. "We can simply get married right now!"

"Right now?"

"Sure. Why not? We know we want to marry, don't we? So why wait?"

So they flew to Italy and got married in the Italian version of the registry office in the town of Gaeta, between Rome and Naples. It was on Italy's romantic Mediterranean coast.

In the spring of 2008, when Katya completes her master's degree, the couple will move to Italy, where Paolo will complete his Ph.D. After that? Well, they will wait to see where God leads them. They have faith that He will show them His will, and they know that they could have no better guide.

They will follow Him, no matter how rough the path may become. And Katya, who for many years sought Olympic gold, has traded that for the gold of the New Jerusalem's streets. Without a doubt, both she and Paolo know that that is the only gold worth striving for.

A Horse Called . . .

Meet five remarkable horses—Mayonnaise, Blackberry, Poppyseed, Tamarindo, and Saskatoon. As you read these exciting stories, you'll learn information that will help you earn Pathfinder honors in Horsemanship and Horse Husbandry.

Book One 0-8280-1131-1
A Horse Called Mayonnaise
JoAnne Chitwood Nowack

Book Two 0-8280-1090-9
A Horse Called Blackberry
JoAnne Chitwood Nowack

Book Three 0-8280-1307-1
A Horse Called Poppyseed
JoAnne Chitwood Nowack
Sequel to A Horse Called Blackberry

A Horse Called Tamarindo
JoAnne Chitwood Nowack
Sequel to A Horse Called Poppyseed
Book Four 0-8280-1499-X

A Horse Called Saskatoon
JoAnne Chitwood Nowack
Sequel to A Horse Called Tamarindo
Book Five 0-8280-1562-7

SOAR INTO A TRUE WILD ADVENTURE!

Rick, Tim, and Marcus can't stop dreaming of becoming mission pilots and buying the ultimate mission plane— a yellow Super Cub. The only problem is that at the rate their allowance is coming in, it will take 63.9 years to raise enough money! As they set out to raise funds, the boys meet up with lots of surprises —from an angry skunk to slashed bike tires, a fire in the woods, and a reckless hang-glider flight. You won't believe the mishaps they encounter—and the lessons they learn along the way—as they set out to earn cash for the plane of their dreams.

0-8280-1919-3

3 Ways to Shop
- Visit your local Adventist Book Center®
- Call 1-800-765-6955
- Order online at AdventistBookCenter.com

REVIEW AND HERALD®
PUBLISHING ASSOCIATION

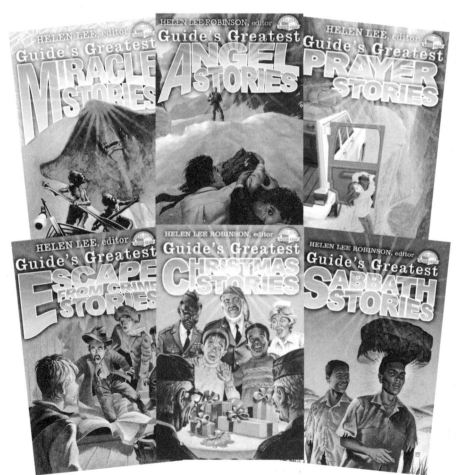